Twilight
Tales

First published in 2019 by Twilight Cat

ISBN 9781912892280

Also available as an ebook

ISBN 9781912892389

Typeset by Clair Lansley

Project management by whitefox

Printed and bound in the UK by Clays

Twilight Tales

Atticus Ryder

CoNtents

The MemoRy ThieF

The mist filled the cave with a colourful glow, its vivid wisps writhing over the ground. Two ice-blue eyes flared open as an orb smashed to the ground, releasing another plume of mist. Two ears twitched in the dark, listening to the whispers of laughter that joined the twisting vapours. He hadn't meant to drop it, but it didn't matter; there were others. The creature jumped up from his rock chair as his lips peeled back in a grin. Click-click-click, his claws clattered, tracing a familiar route across the cave.

The creature scanned the wall of shelves filled with thousands of glass orbs. Glimmering, stacked in pyramids, they were each no bigger than an apple. The creature drifted down the shelves, letting his fingers skip across the orbs, which released bright waves of colour into the cave as the trapped memories came to life at his touch. A dark gap stood out where the broken memory orb should have stood. He rubbed his hands together in glee. *Time to add to my collection.*

⭐ ⭐ ⭐

It was freezing cold in the dense forest, but the creature crept over the ground quick as a flurry of snow. His skin was cold to the touch and darker than the deepest midnight. *Meant for the shadows*, he'd been taught. The trees parted to reveal a clearing with a ring of wagons parked around a large fire. They were made of wood, with curved roofs, and were painted bright reds and yellows. His blue eyes darted around, watching, waiting. His quick, nimble fingers scooped up some snow and squeezed it into a tight ball. Slinking from nook to cranny, he searched until he found what he was looking for – an open window.

After a hop, he grasped the ledge and silently slid into the room. It was warm and cluttered with shelves of toys and books. Chairs crammed around a little table were piled high with clothes. A small brazier cast orange shapes on the walls. In the only bed at the back of the wagon, a blonde, curly-haired child lay asleep under a thick blanket. Placing the snowball gently on the pillow, the creature began uttering the string of secret words.

And then she opened her eyes.

He leapt back and growled.

The girl pulled the covers up to her chin and stared straight at him. 'Hello.'

Narrowing his eyes, he crouched low and tried to look fearsome. The girl giggled as his nose wrinkled and a little growl came out, like a cat's.

'Grrr,' she copied him.

Sighing, he stood up. 'This is just great. A brave

girl!' he said, as she watched and listened. 'I suppose you think I am a common Goblin?' He pointed to his chest.

'No,' she replied.

'Oh!' His shoulders slumped.

'You're the Memory Thief. Mother told me not to be scared of you, because you're lonely. She said that's why you break into people's homes and steal happiness.'

Frowning, the Memory Thief snatched the snowball from the pillow. 'Hmmph. You're wrong! I am very content.'

The girl cocked her head. 'Why have you brought a snowball inside?'

Aha! Now here's a chance, he thought. He placed the snowball back on the pillow and whispered, 'Think of a happy thought. Anything at all – it just has to be happy.'

As he uttered the secret words that had been passed down from grand-thief to grand-thief, wisps of colourful mist flowed from the girl into the snowball. As the flow ended, the snowball shone brightly and then became clear as glass. He picked it up, feeling the familiar weight of a captured memory, and then passed it to the girl. Laughter echoed in the wagon as she held the orb, enjoying the memory she pictured in her mind.

'Here you go,' she offered, handing it out to him. 'You didn't steal this one. It's a gift – from me.'

He looked at her smile, then at the orb, and snatched it up before rolling it over his fingers. A little bit of him couldn't help but think how nice it felt. *No.* He told himself. *It's not right! I'm a thief. Thieves don't receive gifts.* But he kept it all the same, and disappeared into the night.

Back in his cave, he placed the orb on the shelf with all the other memories, then sat back. Suddenly the girl's words popped into his head, *Mother told me not to be scared of you, because you're lonely.*

'I'm not lonely.' he said defiantly.

Then his eyes drifted to the place where he'd put the orb. Was it glowing more than the others, or was it a trick of the light? The cave suddenly felt very big and the chair felt cold to the touch, even for him.

I am a little lonely, he thought. The tiny pinprick of truth threatened everything he thought he knew about himself. Then he looked at all the other memories he had. He was a thief! Being alone was part of the job, and surely it was worth it for all the happiness he had gathered.

'No! I won't look into you,' he said to the new orb, swivelling away.

Still, a part of him deep down couldn't help but wonder what the little girl had given him. Stolen memories were always enjoyable. Could this one be any different? One peek wouldn't hurt . . . he picked it up again. The orb's enchanting glow shone through his skinny fingers. After viewing the memory, he dropped the orb like a hot coal. *It's me*, he realised, *growling in the wagon*.

He took a step back. The girl was full of joy. This wasn't right. He was supposed to steal happiness, not give it. He gingerly picked up the orb and buried it under a pile of memories in the lowest part of the cave. It was time to go out again and steal better memories that wouldn't bother him so much.

Travelling light and fast, the Memory Thief arrived at a town near a small mountain while it was still dark. The town was full of houses nestled together. He could see whispers of memories in the dreams of the sleeping people. His nose twitched. A memory from a boy had a cave in it, just like his. He followed his instinct and slipped down a narrow lane, over a hedge and around to the back door. At the wave of his hand, the lock clicked and the door gently swung open.

In a flash he was standing next to the boy's bed, and pulled out a snowball from his bag. His nose twitched again. The memory was a delicious slice of happiness tinged with a little fear. He looked at the boy's sleeping form. Even in the dark he could make out his blond hair, just like the girl's from the wagon. The thief hesitated, the thought of her haunting and enchanting him all at once. The snow began melting on the pillow. And then, just as he bent down towards the boy's ear, he felt something else. Another memory, leaking from another dream.

And it was coming from next door: an old woman was happily remembering making the boy scrub the floor whilst she ate fat cream cakes. *That's not very nice*, the Memory Thief thought, then snatched up the melting snowball and stole her memory instead.

By the time he had pilfered snippets of happiness from all the neighbouring houses, his side was dragged down by the weight of his pouch. It was time for home. Sitting on the ground back in his cave, he undid the string holding back all the glistening orbs and in quick succession touched one memory after another with a greedy grin.

At first, it worked just like normal, and he felt a burst of happiness as each new memory entered his mind. But then something peculiar happened. The happiness faded away like a wisp of smoke and the clear crystal became a snowball again. *No!* he thought, and nervously grabbed another one, but the same thing happened again – until every new memory he'd collected lay in a heap of snow.

Clenching his fist, he rooted through his

collection at the back of the cave and seized the memory from the girl. It was all her fault, he was sure of it. He held the orb in his hands and tried to work out why this memory felt different to all the

others. And then it came to him. Normally he was just watching someone else's memories from afar, but this one he was a part of. He gritted his teeth, stubbornly ignoring the flicker of true happiness that he felt, and stormed out of the cave.

At the very top of his mountain, the Memory Thief stood poised to shatter the orb on the jagged rocks. This was it – he would be free from the little girl's memory and this feeling that he was part of it. Suddenly, the howling wind whipped the orb from his fingers. Without thinking, he caught it with his other hand and pulled it close. He didn't want to let go. Not yet. He sat down on the cold snow and noticed for the first time that his gift felt warm against his chest. In his mind's eye, he watched the girl smile as he growled. Unafraid, the girl had taken a bit of her happiness and lovingly given it to him. Maybe it wasn't so bad after all. A smile tugged at his cheeks.

After a while, he found himself wandering back through the forest until he came once more to the place where he'd found the wagons. He held the memory close, soaking in its warmth. A white blanket of snow covered the clearing, but there was no trace of the travellers or their fire. Standing there in the quiet and the dark, he slumped against a tree.

Time passed and the Memory Thief stopped stealing. He never went back to his cave. Instead he wandered over mountains, through valleys and across countries. Often the warmth of the little girl's memory guided him gently back to the empty clearing where he had first shared true happiness.

Then, one night, when the winter clouds let the stars peek out, the clearing shone with firelight. The travellers were back. His years of being a watchful memory thief took over. He crouched low, eyes seeking the shadows. Again, the wagons were parked in a circle; he recognised the girl's home and, again, the window was open. After a hop he grasped the ledge and silently entered. He looked around and felt the warmth creeping into his bones. So lovely – just like it had been before.

'Hello, Memory Thief,' said a woman, as she put more wood on the stove.

He scowled at first, but the voice sounded familiar. After a closer look he recognised the dimples in the woman's lined face – it was the girl he knew.

'You're old! I came back before, but you'd gone. Something happened to me when you gave me that memory. I felt content. Tell me how you did it.'

The woman smiled and invited him to sit down. 'It's no secret, Memory Thief. I gave it of my own free will. Everyone knows that giving has much greater power than taking. It's the power of love.'

The woman moved across the room and stopped beside the bed. 'Would you like to meet my daughter?'

She pulled back the thick quilt. Underneath a girl lay with red cheeks. The Memory Thief thought he could maybe see little beads of sweat on her forehead.

'She's been very ill for a long time. It's been a hard road for us. She hasn't had the happiness I had,' the woman explained.

The thief crept closer to the bed and put his orb down on the pillow. 'You should give her some of your happiness then,' he suggested.

'I would if I could, Memory Thief, but I have no way to share my memories with her. Maybe you could help?' The woman reached for his orb.

'No!' he cried, snatching it up to his chest and stepping back. 'You gave it to me and me alone!'

Pausing by the window, he looked at the sleeping girl. *I'd lose my gift and that's not fair*, he tried to reassure himself as he turned to leave. He was sure he was right. But then he glanced back and saw the woman's trembling lip. Now he wasn't so sure.

This was no good! 'I am a thief and that's that,' he announced, and slipped quietly out of the window.

The snow crunched under his footsteps. He stopped, fished the orb from his pouch and rolled it over his hands. He could hear the laughter within it, but he could no longer feel the happiness. It was as though he was looking at it through a window. Setting the memory on the ground, he decided to remember that night for himself. With his eyes closed, only darkness greeted him at first, then, little by little, the images came back: he pictured the brazier crackling, the brightly coloured blanket, the waxed wood under his feet. A tingle went down his back.

'*Here you go*,' the girl offered. '*You didn't steal this one. It's a gift – from me.*'

I don't want to be a thief any more, he realised. *I want to be like her, no matter what it takes.* He took a deep breath and picked up the orb, then crept back into the wagon. The woman sat asleep in a chair by her daughter's bed. Just above the girl's head a small glittering cloud swirled, but as he approached with the orb it disappeared. *How strange*, the Memory Thief thought. But then he focused on the task at hand. He uttered the secret words in reverse, so that wisps of mist flowed from the orb into the girl. Soon the orb returned to a snowball and the gift passed on. Before it melted, the Memory Thief dropped it out of the window and watched as the girl woke her mother with a hug. She looked over at him.

'This is the Memory Thief,' she said. 'He is an old friend from when I was your age.'

The girl looked from her mother to the thief and opened her arms. Gingerly, the Memory Thief walked forward, into her embrace. Then he felt his own arms hold her all the tighter. They talked, and for the rest of the evening created happy memories that would keep him warm inside for the rest of his days.

Before he left, the Memory Thief hesitated. He wanted to see them again, but was too shy to ask. Eventually, he let the words spill out. 'Will you visit me on my mountain sometime?'

'Of course,' replied the girl and her mother.

Then he remembered they'd never been before and might not be able to find him. 'If you ever get lost, I will make the sky glow, so you'll know where to go.'

Once he was back in his cave, he grabbed as many old memories as he could carry and marched up the mountain. At the top, he smashed two orbs together and a mist filled the sky with waves of vivid blues, greens, purples, reds and yellows. And now, when children ask why the night sky glows in winter, they are told the story of the Memory Thief and how he created the colours of what we now call the Northern Lights.

THe Dancing Troll

To boogie or not to boogie? It was a simple question for Albert the troll. It was *all* about the boogie. Boogieing was far cooler than anyone knew. Admittedly, the troll's dance moves weren't the most graceful; if anything, smelling of mould and looking like mud were his specialities. Still, every night he would crack out his twists, shuffles and jumps with

rustling leaves for music and the moon as his disco ball. Sometimes, when it was so cold Albert could see his

breath, bright wisps snaked across the night sky and he would wobble his belly in time with their waves.

You'd be right to ask why he didn't find a dark cave to sit in, eat meat and do what trolls do best – be grumpy. But Albert was different. He didn't grunt; he had a strict 'moss only' diet, so he wouldn't try to eat you; and, to top it off, he was afraid of the dark. That being said, he could be just as grumpy as the best of them. Albert was still a troll, but with a twist.

And twirl, whoosh. And jump, whoosh. Whoooooosh . . . splat. Albert fell flat on his face. He narrowed his beady eyes at the roots that were sticking out from the moss-covered ground.

'Silly, stupid tree,' he grumbled.

Flopping back, he gazed up at the moon through the trees and picked his nose. A shadow zipped across the sky. Albert watched as a dragon's great bat-like wings flapped away in a fluid rhythm. Soon it was gone, leaving Albert to his thoughts.

'If only I could go anywhere, like that dragon,' he sighed, to break the silence. 'I want to be free of this boring forest!'

Then he had a thought. Maybe he *could* leave the forest. Yes! Why not? He could just go, couldn't he? But no sooner had he thought it than questions and doubts began to crowd into his mind. *Should I? What if it wasn't as good as I thought?* He knew of a cousin who went to live under a bridge. Then he remembered what his grandad always used to say: 'The easiest way to get somewhere is to put one foot in front of the other and keep going until you're there.' After all, maybe there were other trolls out there who liked to dance like him!

Albert stood with a jump, puffed out his chest and began to trudge through the forest.

After a day of trekking, his arms hung limp by his sides. He had stubbed his bulbous foot twice and his lumpy body had slipped in mud more times than he could count. Albert stopped in his tracks as his tank of enthusiasm ran down to zero.

'It can't get any worse,' he muttered.

Then a pigeon poop landed right on his head – *splat!* He shook his fist at the sky, then plonked down on the ground and sighed.

'Now it really can't get any worse,' he mumbled.

It began to rain. He rolled his eyes, stood up, stuck out his chest with resolve and continued his march.

After what felt like forever, Albert stumbled across a big grassy meadow. Wildflowers swayed in the breeze, and there were no pesky tree roots to trip him up. It would make a great dance floor! Full of joy, Albert jumped around, making huge dents in the lush grass. Out of breath and exhausted from his trek, he collapsed onto the greenery and fell fast asleep. Hours later, there was a noise.

'Baaa.'

The troll twitched.

'Baaaaa.'

He rolled over and scratched his shoulder.

'BAAAAAAAA.'

Albert leapt into the air and landed with a tremendous thud. He looked around, making sure he had on his grumpiest scowl. Three sets of eyes stared back. Three grass-filled mouths chomped. Three sets of horns pointed towards the troll. He continued to scowl. A stand-off: three goats. One troll.

'What do *you* want?' Albert grumbled.

The goats looked at each other, then nodded to the forest. 'Go baaack to wheeere you belong in the forest. Or eeelse,' they rumbled in unison.

'*You* go back,' the troll countered. He wanted to stay.

The goats' shoulders started to bop left to right. Their hooves clopped and their short tails wagged in time. On every second beat they muttered, 'Baaack.' Before he knew it, Albert had caught the beat and started to shuffle his big belly around and around.

Suddenly he jumped up, his belly rolling, and pointed a finger at the goats. 'You!' he shouted.

And the goats bleated, 'Baaack.'

Then they started to circle each other, stepping in time to the rhythm.

'You.'

'Baaack.'

'You.'

'Baaack . . .'

Foxes, rabbits and badgers poked their heads out from the undergrowth, while birds jostled for a perch on the branches above. At first, they couldn't believe their eyes as they took in Albert's shuffling moves. What was a troll doing here?

Then the goats started a new beat: one-two-three, one-two-three, one-two-three, one-two-three.

Albert kept up his dance while trying to think of a new move. But before he managed to think of one, the goats started a new lyric and a new beat.

'We're-the-best. Haaa. We're-the-best. Haaa.'

Snarls, squeaks and squawks drowned out the new beat as all the animals around began to protest at the goats' chant.

'You're bullies!' yowled a fox.

'Why don't you leave the meadow?' suggested a couple of the braver rabbits.

'Why don't you *all* leave me in peace,' croaked a toad with a frown, as he ambled off to the edge of the forest.

Albert looked at all the fed-up faces. He was getting another idea. He stopped dancing and motioned for silence. This was his big chance. If he could stand up to the goats on behalf of all the animals, he might be able to make the meadow his new home.

He cleared his throat and waited for his heart to

stop beating quite so fast.

'It's clear that the goats believe they are better at dancing than me,' his deep voice bellowed to the crowd.

The goats just looked smug.

'It's also clear that *any* dancing would be better than theirs!' continued Albert, bravely.

Everyone cheered, except the goats.

Feeling encouraged, Albert waited for quiet. 'We all know the goats don't want me here, so why don't we have a dance-off to decide who is the best? The winner can stay in the meadow!'

Another cheer rippled around the animals. Even the goats bleated in agreement.

'Can we join in as well?' another fox asked, her bushy tail swishing in excitement.

The goats turned down their lips and hunched their shoulders, and the fox's tail went flat. So did her ears. She looked at Albert, who felt tingles creep up his hairy back. He'd never known that others danced too. If he won, he could share the meadow's dance floor!

'Of course you can! Anyone can join in,' he

announced, ignoring the goats' frowns. 'If the goats win, I'll go. If I win, then I will stay. If any other animal wins then they can decide. Does that sound fair?'

Everyone nodded.

Albert gave a thumbs-up. 'Let's take some time to practise and we'll meet later today.'

Outnumbered, the goats agreed, then charged off to eat some grass on the other side of the meadow.

Albert put his hands on his hips, pleased as punch. 'This is going to be great!'

While everyone practised, Albert munched more than a few mouthfuls of pillowy moss and thick grass, then settled down for a good old nap. He was in the middle of a lovely dream when he felt a sharp prod. Sleepily, he squinted through the dusk light to see a figure poking him with a stick! It was the badger. All

the animals were standing around him, waiting. *Uh-oh, they're all ready and I forgot to practise!* HIs heart sank down to the bottom of his stomach. *What if I lose?* He closed his eyes for a second and muttered to himself, 'You can do this.'

The troll felt a second badger gently shake his shoulder.

'OK, OK. Where are we doing it then?' Albert groaned.

The group of rabbits gestured to the forest behind the troll. Puzzled, he turned around – then jumped up in shock. While he had been sleeping, the animals had been busy! They had cleared the ground between two trees to make a stage and draped ivy to make curtains. The bushes were now the stage backdrop.

The troll raised his eyebrows, impressed. Then he looked at the red sky and mumbled to himself, 'The sun's setting. Surely they don't want to dance in the dark?'

Maybe the animals heard him, because a fox rose up on his hindquarters and clapped his paws. The air filled with hundreds of bright twinkling fireflies.

The crowd cheered and whooped as a swarm of the flies whizzed around in circles, like liquid fireworks across the stage.

The bushes at the back rustled and parted and a large pin-striped badger appeared. He barked to silence the audience and the dance-off began.

Another badger ushered the troll and the other contestants behind the bushes, arranging them into a queue. Albert lurched to the back to get a good look at the competition. A foxy double-act were the first in line, followed by some jumpy rabbits. The goats were third, looking disdainful.

The cheers on the other side of the bushes died down as the pin-striped badger stepped forward. He twitched his whiskers and cleared his throat. 'Welcome to the Great Forest Dance-Off and here is our first act!' He motioned to the right.

The foxes trotted through the bushes onto the stage, adding their yowls to the cheers of the audience. Albert began to feel nervous. He'd never really danced in front of others. Wringing his hands together, he whispered to himself, 'You can do it!'

On the stage the red bushy tails were a blur as the foxes strode around with swinging bows and tight turns. Albert listened as each step was accompanied by the tuneless yowling of the foxes' supporters. The troll was glued to the performers as they completed three more parades across the open ground and then breathlessly leapt over the bushes to an eruption of applause. It was over.

Next up, the badger introduced the rabbits. They hopped through the leaves in single file and formed a line. Squeaks and nose wiggles of their fellow rabbits in the crowd encouraged them as they started to hop around in synchronised patterns. Four jumped high as two shot forward, while another two hammered their feet on the ground. Albert felt his heart race and began involuntarily tapping his foot as the beat built up. High jumpers crossed in the air to 'ooohs' and 'ahhhs' in the audience. Albert gripped the tree next to him, wondering if he could really compete against such a performance. Then the rabbits at the front doubled back and twirled over the rumbling ground.

As the rabbits neared the end of their act, they all linked arms and started kicking their long feet out left and right as their ears flopped around. Finally, they stood still, stretched out their paws and bowed to the deafening cheers of the crowd. But before they could bow a second time, one of the goats shouldered through them with his buddies following close behind. The badger barked in protest and tried to order them off the stage, but they wouldn't move.

Silence spread across the meadow. The audience of animals looked around, muttering to each other. Albert felt his muscles tense. He wanted to go and stop those bullies, but before he could move, the badger had ushered the rabbits off stage through the bushes with their heads bowed. The troll narrowed his eyes and the audience jeered and booed. The lead goat turned his scowl towards them and moved casually from one hoof to the other.

'We're the billies!' he shouted.

Another goat appeared on his left. 'We're so gruff!'

Then the third goat appeared on his right. 'We're the goats that always say, "Tough!"'

They continued rapping together, all the while bopping from one hoof to the other.

We don't like no troll in our hood.
If it were our say it would be back to the wood.
We're the billies.
We're so gruff.
We're the goats that always say, 'Act tough!'
Foxes and rabbits – think twice.
That troll back there, he ain't so nice.
We're the billies.
We're so gruff.
We're the goats that always say, 'Act tough!'

The act came to an end and the three goats stood there, looking at the crowd. There was no applause. The breeze whistled through the night. After a moment, the middle goat nodded to the other two and they swaggered off the stage. The crowd remained silent.

Albert had been too busy watching to notice someone pushing him onto the stage. He thought of the rabbits and clenched his fist, but then the badger's last shove sent him tumbling through the bushes.

'Whoa!' he yelped.

Catching his foot on a tree root beside the meadow, he nearly fell flat on his face. A muddy end looked unavoidable, but Albert used his weight to turn the tumble into a roll that finished with a leap, his arms reaching up to the twilight sky triumphantly.

He came back down to earth with a thud that rocked the crowd. Swinging his arms wide, Albert bowed to deafening applause. The crowd hushed as he began. Tapping his foot, he signalled to the eight rabbit performers to copy his moves as he started a new rhythm. Next he shuffled his belly and raised his arms to the foxes, who yowled in reply. Finally, Albert spun around to the beat and pointed to the backstage badgers, and their deep rumble joined everyone else's.

It was time to boogie! Albert twisted, twirled and spiralled across the meadow, grabbing the foxy couple to parade left and then hopping with the rabbits to the right. The crowd joined in as the tempo increased with the fireflies twinkling around the dancers.

The whole meadow seemed to be caught up in the fun – until the three goats stormed across the stage to stand in front of Albert.

'We're-the-best. Haaa,' they hollered in time to the beat.

But Albert was ready, and threw a challenge right back. 'We're *all* the best, the best, the best.'

Barks and squeaks joined in with the new song and the dance continued. But the goats refused to dance in time, stomping to their own beat in front of the troll.

Still everyone carried on. To Albert's surprise the goats turned to walk away, across the meadow.

Is that it? Have I won? Albert wondered. He almost felt a bit sorry for them.

And then he felt a solo song rise up out of his chest. 'Stay . . . I am a moss-lover, not a fighter. Stay . . . We can create new raps together.'

The goats paused and then moved into a tight huddle.

After some hushed bleating, the biggest goat looked up at Albert. 'What kind of raps?'

Albert stopped moving, shock rooting him to the spot. He hadn't expected the goats to consider his offer, but now he thought about it, it was a great idea. They could form a club and everyone would win!

'Any raps you want!' Albert offered.

But the other animals had gone quiet. Some of them were muttering. Albert scratched his chin. *Maybe they don't want to be bullied any more*, he realised.

'You'll have to share the grass with everyone and be more patient.' he cautioned the goats.

The goats looked at each other, then, one by one, went over to the troll and shook hooves with him. Albert raised his eyebrows and smiled at the other animals, hoping they'd agree. Tentatively, a rabbit hopped on to one of the goats' backs, and the beat started up. Albert clapped, and everyone danced and rapped until dawn.

Exhausted, Albert curled up under an oak tree and enjoyed the last bit of twilight before dawn. He had found a new home, and, after all, life is a dance that you learn as you go along.

Retry The Fly By

'I *can* fly!' the dragon puffed in desperation.

Whoooooosh. whosh-whosh-whoosh. Oomph.

He tried again with a jump. He flapped his small wings, but it was no good.

Thud.

Finally, he flopped down on the ground and shivered as the rock cooled the scales on his belly. Two jets of steam burst from his nostrils as he sighed, adding more wisps of cloud to the air that gusted around the mountaintop.

He watched the cloud as it swirled and twisted. 'If only I was better in flight school, I'd be able to move like that,' he muttered sadly.

After a time, the clouds parted, revealing the landscape below. The dragon raised his head to look at all the colours that stretched beneath him. There was a thick forest with a sparkling river that led to golden fields and a small village. He watched some birds in a tree below taking a dive from a tall branch and then swooping up into the air. Then he had a new idea!

Waddling back a few steps from the mountain's edge, he stopped and took a deep breath. He dug his claws into the rock, then launched himself as hard as his legs could push. The air whistled passed his horns as he rose up. He was over the edge and sailing through the air. His wings flapped furiously – first on one side, then the other. He stretched, trying to push himself upwards, but it was still no good. That awful sinking feeling filled his belly. *Tumble-tumble-tumble-smack. Tumble-tumble-tumble-smack.*

KA-BOOM!

The dragon opened his eyes. Everything around him was a blur, and then it went black.

Jack sniffed the air. He opened the window wide

and clambered onto the sill to get a better view. Over the rise towards the craggy mountain he could see a zigzag of dark smoke fanning out across the sky. Another puff of smoke exploded into the air, and Jack's jaw dropped as sparks whooshed through the haze.

'What on earth is that?' he exclaimed, a shiver running down his back.

Just then, a group of noisy villagers marched passed his grandmother's front garden with the mayor strutting at their head. Judging by their direction, they were heading through the village square towards the source of the mysterious smoke.

I'm going too, Jack decided. He jumped down from the windowsill and hopped down the stairs two at a time. He was about to dart through the back door when his path was blocked by a hunched figure. Jack hardly dared look up, but when he did he was greeted with his grandmother's pursed lips and stern eyebrows.

'And where do you think *you're* going?' she said in her raspy voice.

Jack's mind raced. *I need an excuse.* He was used

to sneaking out, but this time he hadn't been as careful as normal. He couldn't help remembering last time he'd been caught – she'd made him polish every bit of brass in the house until he could see his face in it.

'Well – I need to clean the front windows so I was just going round the front to check if...' He paused and ran his fingers through his short hair.

'Yes?' His grandmother leaned down and narrowed her eyes.

A flash of inspiration popped into his head. 'If – we had drawn water from the well, so I could clean properly . . . Just as you like it,' he added with a grin.

A bony hand thrust a bucket full of water towards him and grinned back.

Jack groaned. 'But everyone is going through the village square and I want to go, too. Please?'

'How stupid do you think I am? I just caught you sneaking out. I may not be your grandmother by blood, but when I adopted you I made sacrifices to raise you. And this is how you treat me!' She placed her hand on her heart and looked solemn.

'I only ask you to help an old woman and be a *good* boy.'

After years of the same speech, Jack was immune to it. The truth of the matter was that she made him do *everything* around the house – so much so that he barely had time for school.

'Just last week, when my old arms tried to clean the chimney, I got covered from head to foot in soot,' his grandmother carried on.

Jack held back his smile. She still didn't know it was him who had set up the prank after some great advice from a man travelling through town.

'Jack! Are-you-paying-attention?' Her voice went up an octave as she tried to make him feel guilty. 'You-still-haven't-finished-cleaning-under-the-sink. Not-to-mention-the-sweeping-or-the-washing . . . and-don't-get-me-started-on-the-dusting-or-the-gardening. My-windows-aren't-clean! Do you hear me?'

Jack sighed. She wouldn't allow a trip to the village square, that was for sure. The back door was a no-go and the front door was locked. There was only one thing for it. He'd have to find a new escape route. He nodded and wrung his hands together, trying to look at meek as possible.

'Sorry!' he said, hoping she'd at least leave him alone now.

He took the bucket. It was heavy, and water sloshed out of it as he staggered up the stairs. Reaching the bedroom, he lowered it to the floor and then looked around. There had to be a way out! The window was a logical choice, but how would he get down? In the cupboard he noticed a pile of folded white bed sheets and had an idea...

After pulling a few sheets out, Jack tied one in a knot around the bedpost, giving it a tug for good measure. Then he listened to check if his grandmother was near. All clear. Shuffling his bottom up onto the sill, he hauled the sheet up and leant out the window. In the distance he could still see the puffs of sparkling smoke, and his stomach filled with butterflies.

Then the stairs creaked. He froze. His grandmother was coming up. It was too late to hide the sheet. He took a deep breath: adventure called. He scrambled out of the window, holding onto the bed sheet for dear life. Then – he jumped! Luckily, he landed on both feet and sped off down the path towards the gate. He'd done it again! As he looked back at the sheet blowing in the wind, he saw his grandmother shaking her fist at him from the window.

'Jack!' she screamed.

I'll pay for this later, he thought.

The village square was full of people. Jack jumped on the spot to try to see to the front, then craned his neck, but it was no good. Edging left and right, he tried to wriggle through the jostling crowd, but it was too packed, even for him. Jack frowned and listened as best as he could.

'Are you with me?' said the town mayor.

'Yes.' A murmur rippled through the gathered crowd.

'ARE YOU WITH ME?' cried the mayor again, drumming up the momentum.

'YES!' the crowd replied with gusto, some punching their fists in the air.

Jack crossed his arms. He'd thought that everyone was going to investigate the strange smoke coming down from the mountain, not attend some rally in town. A cloud of the fizzing smoke drifted overhead, and one of the tall trees in the green grocer's orchard smouldered as the wisps caught its leaves. *What could cause that?* Jack wondered, with a jolt of fear and excitement.

Suddenly a wave of people started chanting, 'Find it! Stop it!'

Rolling pins, spades, hammers, brooms and the odd candlestick were thrust in the air in time with the words and everyone marched off down the street.

'Finally!' Jack exclaimed.

Then he realised he was still at the back. This was no good! He'd never see the action if he didn't get further forward. As the crowd formed a column along the winding road that headed out of town, Jack ducked through legs and between bodies. In no time at all he was almost at the front and fast approaching the source of the mysterious sizzling smoke. Jack's nose twitched as he breathed in the tangy air. His heart started to race. The crowd grew quiet and people glanced at each other anxiously. They were so close. The mystery fire lay just around the corner. Several *achoos* echoed as another plume of fizzing smoke filled the air. Then they all stopped.

Someone barged past Jack and stepped out in front of everyone else. It was the mayor. He stood as straight as an arrow as he addressed the crowd.

'Now, the thing is – well, the thing…' he stuttered, pointing down the path. 'We, as good honest folk, must stop the thing from whatever the thing is doing.' He paused. '*Achoo!*' He wiped his nose on his sleeve. 'Agreed?'

Jack looked back at everyone's nervous faces.

Clearly no one wanted to answer.

'Are we agreed?' the mayor asked again, sounding ever so slightly desperate.

Jack heard a few mumbles this time, then the village butcher's deep voice piped up. 'What if someone's having a nice barbeque? You know, same as the one last year. That was awfully smoky, too.'

More murmurs rippled around the crowd. The mayor rolled his eyes and beckoned the bulky butcher forward. The crowd parted to let him through and Jack saw beads of sweat on his bald head.

The mayor held up his hands to continue. 'The barbeque was in the village square. Not coming from a mountainside with a suspicious smell.'

'Could be a bonfire?' suggested the town's locksmith.

'Or someone could be smoking a really big pipe,' someone added.

The mayor waved his long-fingered hands for silence. 'We have our families and our homes to think about. Do you want to take that risk?'

He waited for the thought to sink in and the

crowd fell silent.

'Now. Are we agreed?'

'Yes!' everyone reluctantly shouted.

Jack felt the pressure of the crowd behind him as they crept forward around the corner. His eyes grew as wide as the mouth of the cave in front of him, which spread out like a black hole. His heart hammering, Jack felt himself leaning back into the mass of people. Then a low rumble reverberated through him and everyone else as two jets of sizzling smoke erupted from the darkness.

Panicked screams spread quicker than the smoke as more roars vibrated through them. Jack desperately tried to turn on his heel, but there were too many people. Suddenly a stray elbow caught him off balance and he was pushed forwards . . . and then he tripped. Before he knew it he was tumbling down the slope into the darkness of the cave.

His heart in his mouth, Jack sat up. All he could see outside were the backs of the fleeing villagers. Hurriedly, he scrambled up and ran after them.

He dared not look back as another roar made his ears ring. The ground shook. Lumps of rock started falling from the roof of the cave. He dodged left and right. *Almost there.* Then he heard a loud boom and a large boulder rolled across the mouth of the cave. Everything went pitch black.

Jack stood still. Someone – or some*thing* – was breathing close behind him. The hairs on the back of his neck stood on end. He listened in the dark, trembling. Whatever it was, did it know he was there, too?

The dragon sighed. It had all gone downhill since his failed flying attempt. He'd woken up with a throbbing headache and a bruised body. After trying to move, he realised he was stuck. His bottom was wedged into something. To make it worse, every time he strained, a cloud of rock dust filled the cave and made him sneeze. He'd tried one last time to break free. He'd growled and groaned as his claws dug into the ground, but instead of escaping, someone had crashed into the cave to join him.

Then – the roof collapsed.

He sniffed the air and smelt boy. He hadn't come across many humans before. His mother had warned him off speaking to them, but since they were stuck in a cave together he thought he may as well introduce himself.

'Hello.'

'H-he-hello, I'm Jack.' Jack stammered in reply, trying to put his bravest voice on.

Leaning on his foreleg, the dragon thought what to say next. 'Nice day for a visit! Do you, er – well – do you come here often?' he asked.

'N-n-no!' Jack replied, his voice quavering. He was slowly tracing his hands across the wall as he tried to move away from the voice. 'I c-c-came to investigate the s-s-smoke. Never been here before.'

'Oh, I see!' exclaimed the dragon. 'That's my fault. I sneeze when it gets dusty. It always seems to get right up my snout.'

'So you l-l-live here?' Jack asked, after a moment.

'Me, in this shabby cave? I am a dragon! I soar in the sky . . . or at least, I should.'

Jack rubbed his sweaty hands on his trousers. He'd

heard about dragons in story books, but he never thought he'd meet one. Hot breath ruffled his hair. *What if it's going to eat me?* he thought. He began to panic and bolted from where he was standing . . . only to bump into something soft and scaly.

'Omph. Hello there,' said the dragon from above his head.

Jack threw his arms in front of his face in a last desperate act to protect himself. 'Please don't eat me. I'm only a boy. I have to get home. I've got to finish the washing up and wipe the windows and wash the dirty underpants.'

'Eat you? Why, you'd barely be a mouthful. And you smell funny. I don't think I'll be eating you.'

'Really?' Jack lowered his arms.

'Really!' the dragon confirmed.

Jack had never met anyone important, let alone a dragon. Feeling his confidence creeping back, he realised he knew very little about the creatures – only what he'd read, or what other people had told him.

'How come you're here?' he asked.

'Long story short, I fell down the mountain and

now I'm stuck. I was trying to fly.'

'Trying to fly? Does that mean that you can't? I thought dragons were like birds – you know, it comes naturally. A dragon that can't fly – that's just silly!' said Jack.

'Oh, yeah. More stupid than a boy having to clean all the dirty underpants?' the dragon countered.

Jack gave a little chuckle. That was fair.

The two of them continued to chat away until finally Jack offered to help free the dragon, an offer the dragon gratefully accepted. Feeling his way, Jack managed to get to the source of the problem: the dragon's bottom was stuck in an opening at the back of the cave. Just like the cave mouth, it had collapsed into a pile of rocks. Determined, Jack grasped the first rock and started the long process of moving them all.

As he tirelessly moved rock after rock, the dragon kept talking, telling him stories of talking bears and pianos, a dancing troll, the truth about the Northern Lights and a cat he met in a rubbish tip. After lifting a particularly heavy stone, Jack took a rest to get his breath back.

'What's your name anyway? After all, you know mine, and I can't keep calling you Dragon,' he said.

'You wouldn't be able to pronounce it,' the dragon replied.

'Try me!'

The dragon shuffled and cleared his throat. 'My name is De-rik-ew-lele-luska-dora-da-gok...' He took a deep breath, then continued, '...hula-zig-lo-shim-poga-shula-rik.' He paused. 'I guess you could call me Derik for short.'

'It's a pleasure to meet you, Derik.' Jack offered.

'And you, Jack. How's it going back there?' The dragon replied.

Jack noticed there was a tiny blue glow coming from between two rocks in the pile he'd been clearing. It gave him the energy he needed. He grabbed another rock and heaved it out of the way. 'Almost done.'

He had a rhythm now. Grab, heave and throw. Grab, heave and throw. Then, as he hoisted one of the biggest rocks, the small crack opened up and

the glimmering light illuminated the cave.

Jack gasped as he looked at Derik. The dragon was massive – nearly five times taller than him. His scales reflected the light like polished black metal; his teeth were as long as daggers and his tail snaked across the floor. Derik offered a claw to Jack as he saw the wide-eyed boy staring at him. Jack tentatively accepted with his hand, then shook more vigorously.

'You're bigger than I expected,' Jack pointed out.

'My mum used to say that a lot! I guess I'm big-boned.'

Jack nodded. Then a new thought struck him. He

quickly jumped over Derik's tail. While he'd been getting used to the sight of a dragon, he'd completely forgotten the reason he could see it in the first place – the light coming from the opening he'd created. As Jack pulled more rocks out of the way. Derik manoeuvred himself out of the hole, turned himself around, and they both peered through it.

'There's a big drop-drop-drop,' Derik's voice echoed.

'The light is coming from above-above-above. We must have broken into a big crack in the mountain. It's called a fissure-fissure-fissure,' replied Jack.

They looked at each other and then back down at the bottomless dark below. A tremor struck, forcing them to grip the edges of the opening. Urgently, Derik leaned out of the cave and tried to stretch up to reach the top of the fissure, but it was too high and there were no places to pull himself out.

Meanwhile, Jack peered down into the darkness. 'If we can't get up to the light. Maybe we could climb down-down-down? Can you hear that-that-that? Sounds like rushing water down there-there-there? We could follow it.'

Derik nodded his agreement, but before they could move, the ground trembled violently again. The cave ceiling cracked as rocks started smashing down, and suddenly they were dropping, falling through the darkness. They shouted as they plummeted through the black, but the rushing sound was deafening. *Shhhhhhh. Splash! Splosh*!

The water was freezing. Jack rolled and twirled in the river's current, desperately trying to gulp a breath of air, but the world was a dizzying torrent. Reaching the surface, he gasped and blinked the water out of his eyes. Steep rocks rose on either side, so he bobbed along as the current took him. Derik was nowhere to be seen. There was another stomach-wrenching drop, followed by a splash. This time Jack got to the surface quicker, sucking in the air.

Light blasted his eyes as Jack was whooshed out of the cave. As the river slowed, he turned in the water, searching for his new friend, but he still couldn't see him. He managed to swim over to the bank and climb out, then flopped onto the shore. The banks of the river were lush with grass and overhanging trees. Jack looked around again, confident he would soon find Derik, but he wasn't there.

'Derik!' he called.

No answer.

'DERIK!' he called again.

Still no good. After calling one more time, a sinking feeling crept up on him as he ran his fingers through his wet hair and paced up and down the bank. Feeling desperate, he splashed back into the river.

'Derik!' he hollered once more.

The seconds stretched into forever as he waited. He sat on the riverbank for a while, wondering what to do, then trudged back into the water and looked upstream. Three identical red and yellow goldfish gave a 'gloop!', then circled his legs, encouraging him to turn around.

'What's all the shouting about?' said a familiar voice.

Jack turned in a flash. 'Derik! You're here. You're OK. I thought you might have – you know.'

The dragon grinned. 'What an exciting ride, eh? I enjoyed the last drop, and then the swimming. That was really fun. I am a good swimmer if I do say so ...'

The words trailed off as Jack's surprise turn into a frown. 'Exciting? Fun? I nearly drowned! I'm soaked through and I was worried you'd drowned as well. Where have you been?'

Bowing his head, the dragon pointed downstream. 'I was enjoying paddling,' Derik replied sheepishly.

'So where are we now? I have to get home. I hate wearing wet clothes. It's all your fault. If you could fly, we wouldn't be in this mess!'

Derik straightened, reaching his full height. 'Jack!' he thundered, reproachfully.

The boy looked away from his friend. 'Sorry.' Then he offered his hand to the dragon.

Derik slouched back down and gave a firm shake with his claw. 'At least we're out of the cave now, eh?'

The boy watched the lazy flow of the river for a moment. The three goldfish jumped into the air as if to say goodbye before disappearing downstream. Dappled light glittered on the water as the sun dipped. 'You're right. It was fun. I was just scared. I do need to go home though.'

Derik slowly nodded in agreement, stifling a

yawn. Looking around, neither of them could work out where they were, so Jack shimmied up the tallest tree and scanned the horizon, using his hand to shield his eyes from the low sun. Landing back down with a thud, he pointed up and away from the river.

'It's that way! But we'll never make it before dark. It's miles away! I'm going to be in so much trouble when I get home.'

Derik placed a claw on Jack's shoulder. 'It will be OK. We'll walk *really* fast.'

'The only way I could get back before dark is if I flew like a bird' Jack said. He looked Derik in the eye. 'Flew like a bird . . . or a dragon!'

Derik held up his claws. 'Whoa. I'm learning, remember! I jumped off a mountain and I still couldn't do it. I'm not sure I'll ever be able to.'

Jack rubbed his chin. 'You're a dragon?'

'Yes.'

'Dragons fly?'

Derik nodded.

'Good, we're agreed. Do you think either of us is lying?'

'No,' the dragon replied.

'Are either of us crazy?'

'No.'

'Then we must be telling the truth, which means you *can* fly. We just need to work out how.'

Jack ushered the dragon to a clearing, and they began warming up.

They hopped.

They star-jumped.

They did squats.

They ran on the spot.

They leaped from foot to foot and claw to claw.

They lunged.

Derik flexed his wings up and around one at a time, then together.

Now it was time.

Jack climbed up onto Derik's back. 'Remember – I believe dragons fly, which means I believe in you. Let's do it together!'

Derik jogged and then loped until he was sprinting. He barrelled through bushes and hurtled over obstacles: jumping, flapping and falling, but still carrying on. Jack shouted encouragement and Derik felt his heart surge. *I can fly!*

He jumped again. This time he stayed up a little longer before he fell back to the ground.

'You can do it, Derik! You can do it!'

Feeling the power surging through his long wings, Derik jumped, bellowed out a cloud of fizzing smoke and rose up into the sky. Higher and higher he went, sending a stream of smoke into the air. He was doing it – he was flying!

Jack pulled his shirt tight around him. It was colder up in the air, and his clothes were still a little damp. He looked down at the landscape below.

Trees seemed like bushes and lakes looked like puddles. The sun shimmered on one side of the sky, and stars twinkled on the other.

'We're nearly there!' Derik called out.

Jack took his eyes off the night sky and saw the soft glow of lamplight in the village.

'Never had to land before. You might want to hold on,' Derik warned him.

Jack held on tight and tensed his stomach. 'You can do it,' he said to Derik – and himself.

They dropped lower and lower in swift jerks, the ground rising up to meet them. An empty road stretched out ahead. Derik held out his claws, ready to brake, and Jack held his eyes shut tight. *Tumble-tumble-tumble-smack.*

Derik breathed a sigh of relief as he lay on his back with a massive dust cloud behind him.

'Phew. That wasn't too bad, was it?' he called out. But there was no reply.

'Jack?' Derik looked around. Then he heard mumbling and quickly rolled over. 'As I was saying, that wasn't too bad, was it?' he repeated, with a toothy grin.

'Yeah.' Jack wheezed and rubbed his lower back.

They gathered themselves up and crept through the streets back towards Jack's house. It was quiet. Almost too quiet, Jack thought. He hushed Derik as he undid the latch on the back door.

Then a shadow blocked the entrance.

'*So*, there you are!'

Derik retreated into the darkness as Jack stood illuminated by lamplight.

The boy winced. He knew this moment would come, but that didn't make it any easier. 'Yes.'

'Out of the window – and with my *best* sheet! Why, you didn't finish your chores. I had to do everything. Anyway. My-washing-still-needs-doing. Not-to-mention-the-fireplace-or-the-washing-up. I-heard-about-a-cave-and-some-mysterious-smoke-but-that's-not-worth-a-penny-in-comparison.' The old woman paused as Jack looked down. Normally he would just say 'yes' and carry on, but this time, he felt his cheeks burn hot with shame. Here he was being told off in front of his new friend.

'Well, what do you have to say for yourself?'

Jack opened his mouth. 'I…'

'Come on, out with it,' she interrupted.

'I…' Jack tried again.

'Thought so – nothing but cobwebs between those ears. No supper for you! Stupid—'

The old woman's jaw dropped. Derik had stepped into the light, tall and sharp with a small trickle of smoke trailing out of his flared nostrils.

'You were saying?' the dragon challenged. No one was going to bully *his* friend.

'Um… well. Jack is s-s-such a s-s-sweet boy. Always h-h-helpful.' Her lips peeled back into a fixed grin.

Derik raised an eyebrow.

'And of course he'll get supper. I was only joking.' She tried to laugh, but it came out as a tight squeal.

Derik nodded once. 'If I hear even a whisper of you being nasty to Jack, well . . .' He flashed his teeth. 'I'll gobble you up like a ham.'

Jack was rooted to the spot; he wanted to smile and cry all at once. No one had ever stood up for him. He watched in silence as the dragon disappeared into the shadows. He should say something, anything, but that would mean it was over.

Before he knew it, Jack was being ushered up the stairs to his bedroom. The old woman shoved a bowl of thin soup into his hands and locked the door.

Jack placed the soup down and walked over to the window. Slowly lifting the latch, he looked out at the night. *What a day*, he sighed. *I wonder where Derik will go, now he can fly.*

Bed called. Jack started to close the window when he heard a whisper from the garden below.

'Hey Jack, what are you doing tomorrow?'

The boy grinned. 'Hanging out with you!' he whispered back.

'Goodnight,' said Derik.

'Goodnight,' replied Jack.

A Prank Gone Wrong

It was too quiet for the Prankster. All the houses were dark, leaving only the moon to light his way. He hummed a tuneful tune to keep himself company as his shoes clacked down the street.

Quick as anything a stranger appeared from the shadows. His clothes were tatty and his face was covered in grime.

'Money or your life,' muttered the thief.

The Prankster looked him up and down, raising his eyebrows as he noticed the thief wasn't wearing any shoes.

'I said money or your life.'

'I would if I could, but I can't,' replied the Prankster with a grin.

The thief shifted nervously from foot to foot and drew out a small knife. Sweat glistened on his brow and the knife shook in his grip. 'I need your money. And stop smiling at me.'

The Prankster rolled his fingers in the air and then opened his cloak. His fingers made their way towards his waist and moved as if to pull something from his belt. But the thief could not see anything there.

'This, my friend, is a sword,' exclaimed the Prankster. 'A very curious sword. It's so thin it can cut whispers and it's lighter than a feather.'

The thief looked confused. 'You aren't holding anything. Your hand is empty. Now hurry up and hand over the money.'

The Prankster's smile widened. It was true; there appeared to be nothing there. At least to those without the eyes to see it. Carefully sliding the invisible sword back into his belt, he felt a little pity for the thief. 'Ah, just because you can't see it doesn't mean it's not there. After all, a tree falling in the woods still makes a sound, even if we aren't there to hear it.'

The thief boldly waved his knife and threatened again, an edge of desperation in his voice.

The Prankster slowly scratched his chin. 'Do be careful. You might actually hurt someone with that thing, and I am telling you now, that person won't be me.'

The thief shifted again and glanced over his shoulder towards a dark alleyway as the Prankster continued to chat. 'Now, where was I? Oh yes, a tree falling makes a sound,' he mused, absently tapped his chin. 'Doesn't it? Or does it? What do you think?'

'Look, I don't know about trees and I don't have time, either. Please just give me your money!'

The Prankster tilted his head and peered behind the thief. He wasn't sure, but a hunch told him the shadow in the alleyway was another thief who was much nastier than the one in front of him.

'I told you before, my good man – I would if I could, but I can't.'

Out of nowhere, a dirty, hairy brute leapt forward from the alleyway. He pushed past the thief and lunged at the Prankster. Just in time, the Prankster swirled his colourful cloak and side-stepped, letting the brute fall on his face. Taking a moment to haul the dazed man to his feet, the Prankster whipped out his invisible sword and prodded the brute in the bottom. The thief's eyes grew wide when he saw the sword make a dent in the brute's trousers.

'Enough of that, I think,' the Prankster declared, as he swiftly turned on his heel and continued down the street.

Suddenly the thief shouted, 'Look out!' as the brute rushed the Prankster from behind.

But just as quickly as before, the Prankster jumped aside, letting the brute crash head-first into a wall, knocking himself out.

Taking a deep breath, the Prankster bowed. 'My thanks.'

His shoes clacked as he walked on, but then he paused and looked back at the thief. 'I say, you strike me as a decent chap, down on his luck. Thieving doesn't suit you. I have a different line of work available and I've come to the conclusion that you are just the ticket. Come along now. It's dark and you never know who's lurking around the corner.' The Prankster winked.

The thief looked on, openly confused. 'The tree doesn't make a sound because there is no one to hear it!' he shouted after a moment.

The Prankster paused again. 'Good, good. I knew you had an answer somewhere in that head of yours.'

The thief's feet slapped the ground as he caught up. 'Where are we going then?' he puffed.

'Ah, now that's a different question altogether, and it might take more explanation than I can give at the present time. Needless to say, there is a spot of supper in the near future.'

And so off they went, with the retired thief asking questions and the Prankster answering each one with a question of his own. Soon they found an inn where they enjoyed a delicious dinner and went to bed, but not before the thief was made to have a bath.

The next morning, while munching an apple, the

Prankster gave the thief a new pair of shoes and some fresh clothes to wear. They dined on a fine breakfast of bacon and eggs on toast before setting off on the road again. After walking and walking, the Prankster insisted on slowing down so he could have a smoke on his pipe. As billows of purple smoke filled the air, he listened to the story of the thief, who had been named Gerald after his great-great-great-great-great-grandfather.

'I was a royal guard,' Gerald explained.

'Really,' replied the Prankster, his eyes twinkling in the hazy sunlight. 'A guard, were you? Looking after the crown jewels, I bet.'

Gerald stopped in his tracks. 'How did you know?'

'I know a great many facts, my good man, and chief among those is that I am in need of lunch.'

'Is food all you think about?'

'In a word, yes. After all, without food, how can I be expected to think? And how can the world be expected to go on if I am not thinking for it?' He smiled as he produced two ham sandwiches from his pack and gave one to Gerald.

'Enough about me,' said Gerald. 'What about you? And you still haven't told me where we are going and what we are doing.'

'Well,' mumbled the Prankster, with a mouth full of sandwich. 'To begin at the beginning I must answer at the end, and that is to say, we are here.'

'Here?' replied Gerald.

'Here. You asked where we were going. We've arrived!'

Gerald looked around. They were standing in the middle of a dirt road surrounded by fields, with a large oak tree slightly further up.

'As for your last question,' continued the Prankster, 'it's tied up with the first, so that's where I will carry on. I am the Prankster. Paid for my skill, and loved for my art,' he added, taking a bow. 'You may have heard of me.'

Gerald stared blankly.

'I see you have not. So I shall give a simple explanation and all shall become clear,' the Prankster continued. 'I am paid by people to do pranks. You know, replacing the butter with a bathroom soap, bursting a balloon filled with flour, and the like.

There was once a particularly adventurous spider who taught a real corker of a prank with a web...'

But before he could finish, they saw a cloud of dust rising up in the distance.

'Anyway, the answer to your last question will have to wait. We've a job to do. Up that tree we go and not a moment to waste.'

Off he zipped with his cloak sailing behind him as Gerald jogged to catch up. They each grabbed branches and hoisted themselves up onto the thicker branches of the oak tree, then settled high up. The Prankster let out a big sigh and stuffed the rest of his sandwich into his mouth.

Three horsemen came into sight, thundering closer and closer.

Gerald shook the Prankster's arm. 'I recognise the clothing. They're royal guards!'

The horsemen stopped underneath the tree where the hideaways were perched.

'Here, eat this,' said the Prankster, handing over a boiled sweet.

'Why? Will it make me invisible?' whispered Gerald.

'No, don't be daft. It will stop you breathing like a snoring bear.'

'Sorry,' Gerald hissed.

The Prankster smiled and put a finger to his lips.

Meanwhile, the trio of guards had dismounted and gathered around a map that they'd drawn in the dirt.

'If they've come this way, then the only way is along this road,' said the biggest.

'I can't see him,' said the smallest, looking up at the road ahead.

'Might have cut across country,' said the ugliest.

'I am perfectly sure I didn't see him go left,' interrupted the Prankster, as he plopped down in front of the trio.

The guards drew their swords and straightened their clothing.

'Not left, you say. What's your name? Where did you come from? And how do you know who we're looking for?' said the ugly one.

The Prankster looked all around and cleared his throat. 'My name is Gerald,' he announced, emphasising the name of his thief friend, 'and I climbed down the tree.' He motioned with his hands and feet, impersonating his friend.

'You look like a dancing monkey to me,' said the biggest one.

'I said...' The Prankster repeated the phrase, again emphasising the name Gerald and miming climbing down the tree.

Finally getting the hint, Gerald scrambled down the branches as quick as his arms and legs could carry him, trying desperately not to make any noise. The Prankster gave a loud cough as Gerald landed with a thud and crept into the grass beside the road and lay still.

'Look, we don't have time for your monkeying around. We are looking for the thief who took the crown jewels of the kingdom!' shouted the ugly one.

He paused a second, then looked around and up into the tree.

'You!' He pointed to the smallest guard. 'Check up there. Let's make sure this *stranger* isn't up to anything *strange*.' He chuckled at his own joke, but neither of the others dared.

The smallest guard did as he was told, but was

soon back again. 'Nothing there.'

The Prankster took a deep breath and jutted out his chin. 'You are indeed correct, my shorter friend,' he replied, getting a huff of laughter from the biggest guard. 'You'll find that the three of you have been pranked by yours truly, the Prankster.' He flourished his cloak for dramatic effect. 'Your captain wasn't impressed with your attitude on guard duty, and therefore here I am, taking you on a wild goose chase down the road. You've been pranked. There's only me. Aside from my friend in the bushes over there.'

He produced a quill and paper out of nowhere.

'Please sign at the bottom to verify the prank,' he said, thrusting it at the ugly guard.

Well done.

You've been pranked.

Yours in jest,
The Prankster

(Please sign and date below)

DATE: _____

SIGNATURE: _____

'I'd prefer your name but if you can't write, a cross will do. Many thanks and good returns.'

'What if there is a man in the bushes?' said the smallest guard.

'Don't be stupid,' exclaimed the biggest one. 'He is the Prankster. Of course he'd say that.'

The ugly one grabbed the paper and scribbled his name, then walked back to the horses with his companions and they rode off back the way they came.

'Ah ha. Two more silver coins to collect from my friend the captain,' said the Prankster, rubbing his hands together. After neatly folding away the prank receipt, he strolled over to the bushes, offered a hand to Gerald, and they continued walking down the road towards the next town.

Some time later, Gerald plucked up the courage to talk.

'It was me they were looking for,' he confessed. 'And you knew, didn't you?'

'I might have,' said the Prankster, rummaging

in his bag.

'It's how I ended up thieving. I had nowhere else to go.' Gerald stopped and looked at the ground.

With a flourish, the prankster brought out Gerald's 'Wanted' poster. 'Not a bad likeness.'

'But I didn't do it! I didn't steal the crown jewels. I was guarding them all right, but it wasn't me. I got knocked on the head. Then when I woke up everyone was running around and shouting, "Thief! Thief!" So I ran.'

'I know.' A guilty look flitted across the Prankster's face.

'You know?' Gerald questioned.

'I mean, I knew you must be innocent. It's written all over your face. You panicked. Understandable in the circumstances. I shall teach you not to panic, and more importantly, to think.'

Gerald felt his heart lift a little. 'Thanks.'

Soon they reached the town and took a room at an inn. They sat in the corner of the common room playing a game of snakes and ladders in silence.

The Prankster's pipe smoke curled around the egg-shaped counters, each one a bright colour: purple, orange or green. Both of them had nearly made it to square 100 only to slide down the longest snake. The stalemate made Gerald feel fidgety. Their supper sat in front of them, half-eaten.

'Eat up, Gerald. You can't do anything on an empty stomach.'

Gerald sighed, and pushed the food around his plate. 'I want to clear my name,' he announced.

'Yes, I was wondering when you'd come around to that.'

'It's not fair. I had a life before all this. I had dreams.'

'Hmmm,' said the Prankster, chuffing on his pipe. 'But did you pursue them, my good man, or were you living in a stupor?'

'That's not the point!' Frustration reddened Gerald's face.

The Prankster paused to sip some wine, his little finger extended. 'What if I told you you can't change the past, but I might be able to help you rewrite the future?' His eyes twinkled as he put down the glass.

Gerald nodded enthusiastically. 'Yes! I'm in!'

'Good. Now, take that bucket, fill it with water, leave the door ajar and place it on top. It's time for your first prank. We've been paid in advance, and you've just eaten most of the reward.'

Gerald stood up, filled the bucket and placed it on top of the door, as directed.

All the while, the Prankster sat smoking his pipe. 'Now, call the innkeeper,' he commanded.

Gerald cleared his throat and did exactly as he was asked.

Nothing happened.

'Hello?' he said.

Still nothing.

He called out louder. Still nothing.

'EXCUSE ME, IS ANYONE THERE?' he shouted.

Suddenly, the wife of the innkeeper burst through the door and was instantly drenched in cold water.

The Prankster leaped up and grabbed a cloth.

'You foolish pranksters! It was my husband I wanted you to get. Now get out!' she cried. She chased them both outside and threw their belongings after them. '*And* stay out!' she screamed, before slamming the door.

The pair dusted themselves off, but as Gerald walked along, his shoulders drooped.

'Don't fret, my dear fellow,' said the Prankster. 'Learn from your experience. After all, there is no point in avoiding one mishap only to land in another one; you may as well land in both at the same time. It's the shortest way to making sure you don't repeat either of them.'

'Have you ever made a mistake?' Gerald asked.

The prankster scratched his chin and gazed into

the distance. 'Plenty. I would count them on my toes, but I would run out of toes. But whoever said you made a mistake back there?'

The Prankster stopped by an alleyway. And then the innkeeper appeared, smiled and dropped four silver coins into his outstretched hand. Gerald's confusion soon turned to a chuckle and then a laugh as he realised what had happened. The Prankster had been paid by both the innkeeper and his wife to do pranks! He wondered what surprise the innkeeper might find on his return.

'One rule is all I offer,' said the Prankster, setting off down the street. 'Never tell them what prank you will do! It ruins the art and the fun.'

Gerald fell in line and off they went on their merry way.

At first they travelled from town to town, with Gerald learning the tricks of the trade as the Prankster marched on, driven by something that Gerald's questions couldn't quite get to the bottom of. Along the way he discovered his favourite prank

– putting salt in people's tea – and began to feel better than he had done in a long time. Prank after prank, his confidence grew. And after each one, the Prankster produced his receipt and asked for a signature so that he could collect their payment.

But Gerald's thought from back in the inn still nagged at him in their quiet moments: *I want to prove my innocence!*

Then one day, as the sun was setting and they were both feeling very pleased with themselves, the Prankster made an announcement. 'Right, my good and dear fellow. Time to stop!'

Gerald raised an eyebrow, confused.

'You didn't think all that pranking was for nothing, did you?' demanded the Prankster. 'You've been stepping the dance, testing the ropes, finding your voice.' He finished with a flourish of his hand. 'And besides, we've arrived.'

Gerald frowned as he looked at the surrounding forest. It was dense and dark – the kind of place he was warned not to go because of grumpy trolls – and certainly didn't look like any sort of destination. Unfazed by Gerald's blank expression, the Prankster continued. 'We are going to find something that was stolen from me because I borrowed it from someone, who thought they'd loaned it to a friend.' He paused and scratched his chin. 'Come to think of it, that's not even the beginning. Nor the end, for that matter. But we can do what we agreed – we can clear the good name of Gerald!'

With that, the Prankster swiftly nodded and turned away from the path, not giving Gerald a chance to think. Creeping through the undergrowth, the Prankster led the way as the night creatures stirred around them. Step after careful step seemed to last an eternity, until the forest parted and they were faced with a high brick wall. Gerald watched as the Prankster scurried over to it. Seeing a flaming torch above, Gerald dashed after him and pressed his back against the cold stones.

'Where are we?' he whispered.

'Questions later. For now, get the rope out of my bag,' the Prankster ordered.

Gerald undid the strap and reached inside; but instead of touching the bottom, he waved his hand around in empty space.

'Do hurry up. We have a deadline, you know,' the Prankster grumbled.

Gerald reached further until his shoulder was in the bag as well. Then he stuck in his head.

'There's nothing here,' his voice echoed.

'Call for the rope then,' the Prankster offered. 'It should appear on a hook, left-hand side.'

Following the instructions, Gerald found a coil of rope hanging there, waiting. 'Now what?' he whispered.

'Throw it up, of course!' muttered the Prankster.

'But there are no cracks in the wall for it to catch on!' replied a confused Gerald.

'Then say "grip!"' The Prankster shook his head. 'Goodness, what do they teach you at royal guard school these days?'

Gerald threw it, calling "Grip!" as he did so – and the rope hung there, straight as an arrow. He tugged it for good measure; it felt secure, so he pulled himself up, his arms straining under his weight.

'Gerald,' hissed the Prankster, climbing up the rope behind him. 'You know those beans you ate last night? Don't let them out just yet.'

They both suppressed a chuckle and continued to climb. They reached some battlements and came face to face with an astonished-looking guard. The Prankster swiftly drew his invisible sword and clunked the poor man on the head. Wordlessly, the guard slid down against the wall, and Gerald and the Prankster continued along the battlement before turning up a passageway.

Soon they reached a junction and turned left, then left again, always going up. Thinking ahead, Gerald desperately tried to keep track of the route for their escape. They tiptoed past guardrooms, creeping up stairs and peeking around corners. Finally, they found themselves in a chamber that made them both raise their eyebrows. In front of them were doors: an impossible number of doors, covering the walls, the ceiling and the

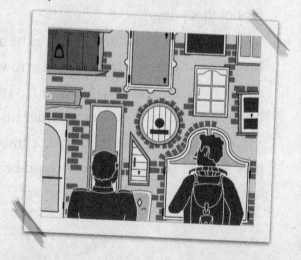

floor. Round ones, square ones, blue ones, barred ones, all waiting to be opened.

'A novel way to distract anyone trying to break in, don't you think?' the Prankster exclaimed.

Gerald scratched his head. *We'll be here all night if we have to try them all*, he thought.

The Prankster paced carefully, avoiding the doors in the floor in case they weren't locked and might send them crashing down into the dungeon. Gerald looked around and quickly tried the handle of the polished metal door next to him. A hairy hand shot out from inside and tried to grab him, but he quickly jerked back and slammed the door shut.

'Not that one,' he sighed.

Next, he tried a little low down one with a brass knob. A small spider scurried through his legs. Gerald could have sworn it said thank you, but then shook his head. *A talking spider? I must have imagined it!*

The Prankster looked up from his deep thoughts and grunted. 'I am at a loss,' he concluded.

Gerald hopped across the room, dodging the same doors as the Prankster had in case they were traps. 'If I wanted to hide something, I'd want to distract everyone as much as possible,' he said, approaching a wooden door, 'by placing lots of stuff around something very ordinary.'

He pulled on the handle of a very plain-looking door. 'There you go!' he said, holding the door open.

The Prankster beamed and patted Gerald on the shoulder, and they entered a room. There were open books everywhere and maps were scattered on a big wooden table. A large window let the moonlight in, and through it there was a view of the forest they had just come from. A painting of a man with dark hair hung on the far wall; dressed in armour, he looked handsome, but mean and selfish.

The Prankster approached it. 'What we are looking for is behind this,' he said.

He slid the painting to the side to reveal a hole in the wall. A black velvet bag lay on its side, tied up with a knot. Next to it rested a small rectangular block. It seemed to reflect light like polished metal, yet it hardly weighed a thing in the Prankster's palm. He examined it closer; the top seemed to have an impression meant for a thumb. When he touched it, a faint orange light pulsed from one corner of the block. He was intrigued by the curious contraption, but there was no time to lose; he pocketed it, promising himself he would look at it more closely later.

Now, his fingers twitched as he reached for the real prize of the evening. The bag was heavy and its contents softly jangled.

'What are we taking?'

'Nothing and something,' started the Prankster, but Gerald interrupted.

'Oh, stop your twiddly words. What is it?'

'Jewellery,' the Prankster replied, flatly. 'Special jewellery that must be returned.'

Gerald's thoughts joined the dots, quick as lightning. 'It's the crown jewels, isn't it?' he shouted, jabbing his friend with his finger.

The Prankster shifted and looked at the ground. 'Well, it is definitely some…'

'Now don't start that again. Yes or no.'

'Yes,' the Prankster confirmed, meekly.

Gerald's face went pale. 'It was you! You're the

thief. You knew which door to take all along. You're the reason I lost my job. My life.' He shook his fist as the Prankster cowered in front of him.

'No! I am not a thief, Gerald,' the Prankster insisted. 'I placed too much trust in a cruel man who was clearly out for himself.' He turned towards the window. 'Truth be told, I was pranking the King. It was going to be my crowning achievement – if you'll forgive the pun.' He turned and winked at Gerald. 'I was going to hide the crown jewels under his bed at the request of the Queen, but they were stolen from me by the same man who knocked you on the head.' Gerald watched as the Prankster shuffled something under his cloak. 'I need you to help me now, and I promise it will help us both in the long run. Will you trust me one more time?'

Gerald sighed, and slowly nodded.

'You'll have to pretend to be me. You'll need to look the part, so here you go,' said the Prankster, handing over his cloak. 'And remember, don't show your face.'

Gerald took the cloak and wrapped it around his shoulders, fastening the clip at the front. He looked up to see only an open window. He was alone. Pulling the hood of the cloak over his mop of hair, he couldn't help but admire the workmanship of the fabric. Gold thread glistened against rich greens, reds and oranges. The inside was lined with something heavy. *Chainmail?* But who would need armour in a cloak?

As he fiddled with some of the hidden pockets, he felt a rush of cold air sweep up his ankles. The door had been silently opened. He dared not turn in case he gave himself away.

'Show time,' he whispered. Remaining still, he tried to hold the velvet bag close. The moonlight almost fixed his shadow to the spot.

'I'm afraid there'll be no show tonight,' boomed a deep voice from across the room. 'Now, be a good prankster and place the jewels where you found them.'

Gerald moved slowly towards the wall, careful to keep his back to the stranger.

'Now, none of your tricks. I am well aware of what you can do,' said the voice. 'Show the contents to me first.'

Sweat trickled down Gerald's back. He untied the knot and flashed the jewels inside, dread filling his heart. If the jewels were still here, how would he clear his name? Surely this wasn't what the Prankster had intended. His breathing quickened as he forced himself to calmly place the jewels back on the ledge behind the painting.

'Good. Now slink off to the hole you came from and don't come back. Next time I see you, I'll make sure you meet a slow and painful end.'

Gerald didn't need any more reasons to leave, but he silently made a vow to come back and get those jewels. He whipped around, careful to hide his face, and made for the door. Sneaking a look at the thief, he saw a cruel smile twisting a bearded face. Then he felt a sharp kick from behind, pushing him on his way, as laughter echoed in his ears.

Running back the way he came, Gerald crept past guards and finally made it outside. Walking as fast as he could without running, he strode through the forest. Then, all of a sudden, a wave of tiredness hit him. What should he do now? Wait, or keep on going? Where was the Prankster? He felt close to panic.

A shadow moved through the trees.

'He'd never have believed it wasn't me that stole the crown jewels, unless he caught me in the act,' said the Prankster, swishing the bag of jewels in front of Gerald.

'You've got them!' Relief washed over Gerald as he sagged against a tree. The Prankster must have switched them when he wasn't looking. 'But why did I have to do it? I got kicked! And I had to run for my life.'

'You've got to start somewhere. All the rest of the pranks were training. This was the serious stuff. So there you go. I declare Gerald a fully-fledged prankster, ready to take on the challenges of further pranking. All you'll need along the road is a dash more cheek, followed by a smattering of cunning and a large dollop of genuine fun.' The Prankster winked.

Gerald smiled, but still felt uneasy. 'What if he checks the velvet bag?'

The Prankster got out his pipe and lit it, letting the blue smoke curl into the air.

'He won't. He's too full of himself,' he replied.

'Right now he'll be congratulating himself on scaring the wits out of me. He's a nasty piece of work, that one. I found out it was him after a bit of investigation. Know your enemy, as they say.'

Gerald took a deep breath. 'Time to get going then,' he declared, putting one foot in front of the other.

The Prankster followed with a slight smile tugging at his mouth. 'Indeed Gerald, indeed.'

After a long, hard journey, tracing their steps back to where they had first met, the pair were tired out, so they decided to hire horses. And this was how they entered the King's palace – on fine mounts

with leather saddles, sitting with straight backs and raised chins.

'I say, Sir Guard. We gentlemen request an audience with the King, if you'd be so kind,' announced the Prankster. Then he gave a quick wink to Gerald and rummaged in his bag. 'The King will also want to read this note.'

The bored guardsman looked at the pair and snatched the note. 'Wait here,' he grunted. Gerald breathed a sigh of relief that the guard hadn't recognised him.

Half an hour later, the pair were escorted to the throne room by ten guards. It was filled with lords and ladies, all watching as the companions approached the King.

'If it's not the world-renowned Prankster,' greeted the King. 'Welcome.'

'Your Majesty is too kind. If I may be so bold, here is my companion and loyal servant to the Crown, Gerald.'

Gerald swiftly bowed, hiding his red cheeks.

'Your Majesty, my profound apologies to you and your family. I fear your loss of the crown jewels was a prank gone wrong on my part. There are two innocent men before you who seek your justice.'

As the Prankster continued to explain their story, Gerald scanned the crowd of bystanders and couldn't believe his eyes when he saw who was standing at the King's right hand. It was the thief!

The story finished, the King stood up and collected the crown jewels from the Prankster. 'Indeed, Prankster. I confirmed your story as soon as I read your note. You shall have your freedom and Gerald shall be reinstated. But I am still displeased, for who did the thieving?'

'I am certain Your Majesty is well aware, after reading my note,' replied the Prankster, careful not to look in the direction of the thief.

However, Gerald couldn't take his eyes off the man at the King's side, who must be his adviser, and saw how he stiffened as the Prankster spoke. Suddenly and without warning, the King's guard rushed forward – but it was too late. The advisor had drawn his sword and was advancing on the King. Everyone gasped. Without a second to lose, the Prankster reached into his bag and whipped out a juggling ball. He hurled it across the room, smacking the advisor right on the nose. Quickly the guards pinned his arms behind his back and escorted him out. The room fell silent.

'Thank you.' The King quickly took control again. 'The Crown owes you a debt, Sir Prankster. Some of those jewels were a gift from a neighbouring kingdom, and I'm certain the thief aimed to profit from any discord. One last question before you go.' He smiled. 'Who commissioned the prank?'

And just like putting on an old coat, the Prankster settled into a comfortable position, foot out and arm raised. 'Ah, Your Majesty, I am afraid a professional such as myself could never say it was the Queen!' he grinned, with a gleam in his eye.

The King laughed and laughed, and then everyone else laughed, too, then the pair finally bowed and took their leave.

Outside in the warm air the birds were chirping and for the first time in a while, everything was right with the world.

Taking a deep breath of freedom, the Prankster turned to his friend. 'Are you coming with me, Gerald?'

'Coming with you?' he replied. 'No. You nearly got me killed twice. And it was all your fault in the first place.'

The Prankster's shoulders drooped. 'Oh. Well, I understand. Good fortune then… to you… and your family.'

Then Gerald caught his arm. 'Ha. Pranked you! Did you really believe I wouldn't come along?'

'Would you like the long answer or the short answer?' asked the Prankster.

'Short,' replied Gerald with a grin.

The Prankster looked slightly disappointed. 'Well done. You got me.'

And the two friends went off, on their new mission to prank where pranks had never been heard of, and to find something that everyone seeks, but few find – a life filled with the simple pleasures.

Junk Town

'Come on, hand him over,' Errol's father ordered patiently.

Errol glanced up at his parents' stern faces. Each wore clothes that matched the curtains and carpet, colour-coordinated and neat.

'Do what your father says, Errol. I know it can be hard. How about playing with your soldiers instead?' added his mother.

The chest at the end of Errol's bed overflowed with toys, but none of them were Swift. In the draughty mansion Errol called home, Swift – a wooden horse given to him on his birthday – was his only friend. The horse's mane was threadbare, he was missing his saddle, his paint was chipped and now his leg was broken; the wood felt jagged in Errol's palm.

His father gently gripped his shoulder as if to say *let go*, but Errol shook his head. *No!* He wished his parents would go back to adult things downstairs. They always told him they were too busy running the local town when he wanted to play.

His father sighed. 'Errol, you know the rules. Old is old and new is better. We'll get you a new Swift, I promise.' Errol swallowed the lump in his throat as he slowly handed over Swift and his broken leg. His parents quickly passed it along to a waiting servant and whispered, 'Junk Town.'

Once they'd left, Errol leant on the window sill and stared at his reflection. His straight brown hair was as flat as he felt. Watching the mansion gardens below didn't help. They were quiet, and the tidy paths with the fenced lawn reminded him of the rules his parents made him obey. Everything had to be new and neat. A door slammed downstairs as the servant who had taken Swift quickly walked down the garden towards town. Errol perked up. Was this his chance? Could he follow him and sneak Swift back into the mansion? The servant disappeared through the side gate.

Errol's body tingled. As fast as he could, he put on a pair of black socks like the wizard in his favourite story, then pulled on some new brown shoes. His old tutor was snoring in the room next to his as he crept by, then down the narrow servant's stairs and out into the garden.

'No running. You'll make my path too dusty!' a gardener shouted.

Errol waved his hand in an apology and then, at the gate, he spotted his target. Quickly, he followed.

The town's high street was busy with people going about their daily tasks. All the houses and shops were set back from the road, and their windows gleamed in the morning sunshine. They were painted bright pastel greens, yellows and pinks. A shopkeeper put a sparkling sign in front of her display, saying, 'New Today!' Errol noticed the quick and nervous glances of a few townspeople as they dusted surfaces that were already clean – yet another reminder of the same strict rules followed by his family. Men with black sacks walked through the crowd picking up litter, and snatching anything that looked a little worn from the passing crowd. Errol's horse, Swift, would be in one of those black sacks if they found him. Errol's heart sank a little. He felt pushed into a mould that didn't fit him. Soon the servant, with Errol following, left the last streets of the town behind, and began climbing the surrounding hills. They were covered in thick scrub and Errol crept from bush to bush, confident he was doing the right thing. But then doubts began to creep in. He'd never been to Junk Town. His tutor's heavy voice wormed into his mind as he remembered one of his lessons: *Junk Town, my boy, is a graveyard, and nothing like our lovely town. It's a resting place for old, unwanted and broken things. It is over the hill because no one wants to see it. It's up to you to uphold the rules after your father is gone. Old is old and new is better.*

Stopping for a second, he looked back towards home. The town was positively gleaming in the sunshine. It was a perfectly polished place. He knew he should like it, or at least that's what everyone told him. He bent down and rubbed a bit of soil between his fingers, breathing in the earthy smell.

The dirt caught in the tiny grooves on his thumb. He imagined his mother's disapproving frown, but something inside him liked being in touch with the world, whatever the rules might say.

Fond memories of carrying Swift up trees, rolling in the grass and splashing in puddles reminded him of what he was doing here. The servant was still just ahead. Taking a deep breath, Errol stepped over the crest of the hill and headed down into Junk Town. The dirt track was dry, and small wisps of dust rose around his feet. Errol scanned the big piles of objects at either side. Everything imaginable was here, from shattered tables to smashed plates, threadbare carpets, rusty pots and pans, discoloured paintings, bent knives, flat tyres and old clothes. The track twisted through the cluttered maze, and the servant disappeared whenever he turned a corner. Errol's heart thumped as he crept through the eerie silence.

Suddenly he stopped, and frowned. A crossroads – and no sign of the servant! *Which way should I go?* he wondered, panicking. Checking left and right, he spotted a hunched figure for a second, then it ambled away to the right. 'I didn't think there were supposed to be any people in Junk town,' Errol muttered.

Curious, he edged closer, watching and listening. 'What do you think?' said the old man, holding up a broken chair. Errol stayed silent as the backpack on the old man's shoulder opened and a cat poked its head out. Its fur was ginger with streaks of white and its eyes didn't match – one was green, one blue. 'Well?' The old man lifted the chair a little. 'Meeeeeow,' replied the cat. Errol watched as the old man tugged his grey beard. 'OK, so you don't like the chair. What about this, then?' He showed the cat a grimy copper kettle. 'I once did a great prank

with a kettle in my younger days. I took some salt…'
He paused. The cat licked its paw and washed. 'Are
you ignoring me now?' Slowly the cat looked at the
kettle and gave it a curt nod. Dusting off his jacket,
the old man shuffled onwards, kettle in hand.

Maybe the old man can help me find the servant,
thought Errol. He felt silly calling out, so he just
trailed after the pair, inching deeper into Junk
Town as he built up his courage. Like a mountain
range, stuff rose and fell around them in craggy
piles. No plants seemed to grow in the dry, dusty
dirt, so when Errol saw a thick leafy oak tree he
hurried towards it to investigate. Peeking around
the trunk, he saw a garden – and it was just as lovely
as his parents' garden! The grass was lush with a
sprinkling of wildflowers, all swaying in the breeze.
A stream glittered as it wound its way through.
Somehow this place made the jumbled-up piles of
stuff seem smaller.

'How can this be in Junk Town?' Errol exclaimed.
Beyond the garden stood a house made of a
patchwork of bricks, plaster, tiles, thatch and wood.
A tree blossomed out of a crumbling stone tower

and the windows were all shapes and sizes. Washing fluttered on the line as the old man disappeared inside.

Errol leant against the tree trunk. Should he follow? Or should he just go home and forget the whole thing? He found himself heading forward, dodging through the grass. He hopped over the stream and stood at the front door; but just as he held up his hand to knock, the door creaked open.

Errol peered through the dappled light. There was a coat rack and odd pairs of shoes were placed next to each other in a tidy row. The old man sat at the table polishing the copper kettle.

He looked across at Errol and smiled. 'I wondered

if you'd pluck up the courage to come in. Welcome to my home.'

Errol inched inside the doorway.

'Would you like some tea and biscuits?' The old man pulled out a chair. 'I've got some rather tasty ones from this morning. The baker threw them out because they were the wrong shape, but they all taste just as good to me.'

Errol's mouth watered as a plate of misshapen biscuits was put in front of him. 'I'm not allowed sweet things. Mother said they are bad for my teeth.'

The old man raised his eyebrows as he poured out a steaming cup of tea. 'Surely one won't harm, especially if you brush your teeth. My name is Old Man Ferris, by the way, and this is Emerald.' He pointed to the comfy chair next to the fire, where the cat was now curled in a ball. The cat's eyes opened a crack and then she went back to her nap. 'Who might you be?'

'My name is Errol,' the boy mumbled through a biscuit. 'My parents told me not to come to Junk Town, but I had to because…' He placed the remainder of his biscuit down and explained who his parents were and what had happened this morning.

Old Man Ferris sipped his tea, glancing over his cup. Then he smoothed down his beard, clicked his fingers and stood. Emerald trotted over to his knapsack and made herself comfortable inside. 'I guess we'd better see if we can find Swift, then.'

Errol got up and tried to slide a biscuit off the plate, then held back as he remembered his parents' frown.

'Take two or three if you like. Make sure you brush your teeth, though,' Old Man Ferris called back with a wink as he strode out of the front door. Piling three biscuits in his palm, Errol followed him out of the door. They traced their steps back to the crossroads, where Old Man Ferris stopped and stroked his beard again. Emerald popped her head out of the knapsack, sniffed the air and meowed.

'Really? You think the servant went that way?' Old Man Ferris asked her.

The cat meowed again.

'Sometimes I wonder how you know what you do, Emerald.'

'All I hear is meowing,' said Errol, puzzled.

Old Man Ferris chuckled. 'Of course you do. Sometimes that's all I hear as well. You'll understand Emerald when she wants you to.'

The old man pointed forward and off they went again. Soon they were searching on either side of the path. As they lifted odds and ends, Errol began to get nervous. What was he doing? A wave of dread washed over him. If he found Swift, his parents and tutor would know he'd been here – *if* they found the horse, that is.

He was putting back an old cushion when Emerald meowed again. The cat had been sniffing inside an old wardrobe. Old Man Ferris sieved through a bin bag sitting at the bottom, and made a low whistle as he slowly pulled out Swift. The horse was covered in dust and his mane was matted with porridge. 'He is so dirty,' Errol whispered. Were his parents' rules right after all? Was new better than old?

As Old Man Ferris examined the horse's broken leg, despair cast a shadow over Errol.

It was no use. 'I…' He hesitated. 'I have to go.' And turning on his heel, he sped off.

Old Man Ferris called out, but Errol kept running and was soon at the crossroads and beyond. He didn't remember the journey back – only relief at seeing the side gate. Locking his bedroom door, Errol sank to the floor and tried to forget the whole thing. But it wasn't that easy. His toy soldiers didn't gallop like Swift, his building blocks didn't take him on adventures and every time he looked outside, his eyes were drawn to Junk Town.

Late that night, when everything was quiet, Errol's thoughts strayed to Old Man Ferris. He felt terrible that he'd left without saying goodbye. Then an idea popped into his head. *I could go and say sorry!* After all, his parents wouldn't want him to be rude.

The next morning, Errol told his tutor he wanted to do his reading time outside. And then he set off for Junk Town. Reaching the crossroads, Errol stepped towards the right, and stopped. Emerald sat in the middle of the path, staring at him.

'Hello. Have you come to help me?' Errol smiled sheepishly. Emerald continued to stare.

'I'm sorry for leaving without saying goodbye,' Errol added. Emerald blinked and remained still as a statue. 'Thank you for helping me find Swift,' Errol said, finally.

Nodding once, the cat got up and trotted off down the path. Errol caught up and fell into line until the oak tree came into view. Hopping over the tree roots, he saw Old Man Ferris on his hands and knees, planting new flowers.

'Ah, I wondered when you'd be coming back!' Old Man Ferris beckoned. 'Time for a tea break.' All three of them went inside. Old Man Ferris put the copper kettle on to boil, and Errol sat at the table next to a wonky sponge cake.

'Cut a slice for each of us,' encouraged the old man. 'Extra butter icing for Emerald. She'll get grumpy otherwise.'

Then, after wolfing down a slice of cake with a few slurps of tea, Old Man Ferris smoothed his beard.

'There was something I was supposed to remember. Ah yes, that was it.' And off he went to rummage in one of the cupboards.

He asked Errol to close his eyes and hold out his hands. Errol's heart leapt. He dared not hope. Then he opened his eyes.

'Wow!' he gasped.

Swift was resting in his hands. The leg was fixed, he had a new coat of paint and his mane was brushed through, glossy and thick.

'Thank you!' Errol shook Old Man's Ferris's hand, scratched Emerald behind the ear and galloped around the room. Finally, out of breath, he plonked himself down again. 'Do you think I could stay for a bit longer and have some more cake?'

Old Man Ferris smiled. 'Of course. As it happens, I'm in need of a hand to help me repair this clock. It's lost its tick and its tock!'

As they repaired and talked and ate cake, the sun travelled across the sky. Errol tidied the plates away and noticed some cobwebs next to the kitchen window. Instinctively, following the lessons from his cleaner, he found a duster and went to sweep them away.

But Old Man Ferris stopped him. 'Oh, leave that if you don't mind. My friend Herbert wouldn't be at all pleased if you removed his home.'

Soon it was time for Errol to return to the mansion. He left Swift with Old Man Ferris so that no one would ever find out that he'd found him. Thankfully, his tutor had fallen asleep and hadn't noticed that Errol had disappeared for half the day.

From then on, Errol would secretly visit Old Man Ferris in Junk Town every morning during his reading time, going on adventures with Swift and learning how to repair all manner of things. But then, one morning in the school summer holidays, when Errol was dashing down the high street, a group of children called out to him.

'You're the boy from the mansion,' shouted a girl. 'What are you doing here?'

Errol froze. He couldn't possibly say where he was going. 'Nothing,' he replied.

'I saw him go to Junk Town yesterday,' said a boy.

'Junk Town!' they all exclaimed.

Errol felt his cheeks heat up. 'What if I did?'

'Can we come too?' the girl asked excitedly. 'It's

boring here. We can't play because everyone wants us to clean.'

Errol's heart beat faster and a hundred questions raced through his mind. He'd never really spoken to any of the children in the town before. He looked at their eager faces and realised how much he wanted to share his secret adventure.

'Sure. Follow me. I'm Errol, by the way.'

As he led the group deep into Junk Town, everyone got quieter and quieter until they reached the oak tree. Then they gasped as Old Man Ferris's garden came into sight. Seeing Emerald in the window, Errol waved and pointed to his new friends.

Old Man Ferris came outside with a large plate of flat scones and a fold-up table.

'Welcome, everyone,' he called out. 'Errol, be a good chap and get some chairs from inside.'

Emerald strolled across the garden and rounded up the children. Old Man Ferris poured some tea and cut up the scones while Errol brought the chairs out and introduced everybody. In no time at all, the children were laughing and chatting.

'What are you doing in Junk Town, sir?' asked

one of the children after a while. 'Our parents tell us it's forbidden.'

'It's quieter here than where you live, and I get a chance to repair things.'

The children gasped.

'You've been fixing the broken stuff?' exclaimed a girl. 'But that's against the rules.'

Old Man Ferris grinned. 'Everything deserves a second chance, and it's wasteful to always throw things away. I was hoping to sort it all out, but it's proving a challenge for my old legs.'

Errol sensed the nervousness of the other children as they glanced at each other. 'It's OK. Really. It's actually fun repairing things,' he said. 'Look at my wooden horse – he was broken once.' He pulled out Swift to show them.

'Maybe you could all help me?' said Old Man Ferris. 'Just like Errol here.'

One by one, the children looked at Errol and nodded in agreement. A few moments later, Old Man Ferris had them all gathered around a pile of junk. Then he showed them how to glue, sand down, polish, tinker and fiddle until all the things were fixed.

Errol patted Swift and looked around at his new friends, then relaxed back in his chair. He couldn't remember ever feeling this happy before.

As the days turned into weeks, the group of children began bringing their brothers and sisters along. Fed up with cleaning and curious about what their children told them, parents went along too. Then they in turn invited *their* friends, until almost everyone from the town was helping Old Man Ferris. The Junk Town path got wider and wider as the broken things were repaired and taken back to people's homes. The baker set up a free food stall for the hungry workers, and Old Man Ferris wandered from person to person, offering advice and encouragement.

Then one day, when the sky was particularly cloudy, a murmur rippled among the people, and everyone stopped work. Silence fell; all you could hear was the dust swirling along the streets.

Errol and Old Man Ferris strained to see who

was approaching – and to his horror, Errol heard a familiar voice.

'Arrest him at once!' his mother commanded.

Two mansion guards stomped over, their expressions grim, to grab Old Man Ferris. Everyone gasped, and Errol quickly hid.

'You're to be charged with disturbing the peace,' said Errol's father. 'All this recycling—' he waved at the repaired objects, 'is strictly forbidden.'

People began to shuffle, glancing at each other and the things they were holding.

'As my father said before me, old is old and new is better!'

But no one cheered like they used to. Now they knew the value of fixing things. Errol's father turned to leave and the guards frogmarched Old Man Ferris back towards the mansion.

Errol gripped Swift, and tried to stop shaking. *This can't be happening*, he thought. No one stepped forward to stop his parents, so he took a deep breath and revealed himself.

'Father,' he shouted. 'Please stop. He was only trying to help. It's my fault really. I invited everyone.'

Errol's father stopped and replied flatly, without looking back, 'You should have known better.'

Errol swallowed. 'But…'

'No buts. Come home,' his father commanded. Errol's cheeks burned with shame as he did as his father told him.

Back in his room, he held Swift close, wishing they could gallop away. And then, without warning, his parents burst through the door.

Errol's mother fixed her eyes on Swift before Errol could hide him. 'I thought we'd got rid of that toy,' she snapped. 'Hand it over!'

Anger burned deep and hot inside Errol. 'No!' he shouted.

His father's face went white. He snatched Swift, but Errol clung on. Suddenly, there was a loud crack and Swift clattered to the floor. Errol held one leg and his father held another.

A coldness settled in Errol, freezing his anger into sharp icicles. His parents silently gathered up the bits of Swift and left. Errol stared out of the window towards Junk Town. That was it. He was sure now.

That night, as Errol snuck out of the mansion, his father hunched over Swift, turning the broken pieces over and over in the firelight. He sighed as he slotted the broken bits together and then pulled them apart again. Swift meant a lot to Errol, and Errol meant a lot to his father. For the first time in a long while, he decided to follow his heart and not the rules. He stood up and went to see someone who could help.

Old Man Ferris was sitting on a wooden bench behind the iron bars in the jail. A lamp flickered in the corner, casting long shadows.

'You can leave us.' Errol's father ordered the guard. Then, once the door was closed, he cleared his throat. 'Old Man Ferris, can you help me repair Swift?'

The old man smiled. 'I can't help you, but I do know someone who can. Why don't we go and find him?'

Finding Old Man Ferris's house in the dark wasn't as easy as Errol thought, but eventually he made it. The door creaked as he slipped inside.

'Hello? Emerald, are you there?' he whispered

Emerald stretched her back legs and jumped on to the table. 'What do you want?' she replied.

'I… I can understand what you're saying!' Errol exclaimed

Emerald began washing herself. 'Correct. What do they teach children these days? Now, what do you want?'

Errol scratched her behind the ear. 'I need you to help me get Old Man Ferris out.'

'I had a feeling you'd say that,' Emerald replied, in between purrs. 'But he is more than capable of getting himself out of this pickle. He was always getting himself into sticky situations when he was younger – playing pranks on everyone.'

Errol found a lamp on the table and turned it on. He was about to try and persuade Emerald to help with his plan when the door creaked again.

'Who's there?' he hissed.

'It's us,' the children from the town whispered. 'We saw you sneaking in here.'

Errol ushered them over to the table and Emerald

purred as the children gave her lots of strokes. Then he talked them through his plan to rescue Old Man Ferris from the mansion.

They scribbled ideas and plans on a big piece of paper, while, despite herself, Emerald offered advice and helped them practise sneaking through the doorway until they felt ready. Placing their hands in the middle of the table alongside the cat's paw, they swore an oath of secrecy.

Then someone knocked on the door.

They froze.

Another knock.

Errol felt his legs wobbling. If he jumped out of the window now, he could escape and carry out the plan alone.

Another knock.

'I say, it's not often you have to knock on your own front door!' said a familiar voice.

The children looked at each other in surprise. Emerald leapt over to the door, stretched up and pulled down the handle. A second later, Old Man Ferris stepped through the doorway, smoothing down his beard.

He grinned. 'I have a guest I would like you all to meet.'

Errol's father came inside and timidly shook everyone's hand. Errol dodged away and put some tea on to boil, while Old Man Ferris settled at the table and asked the children to explain their cunning plan.

'It was all Errol's idea really,' began one of them.

'I thought of the distraction bit!' chimed in another.

'I wanted to use face paint,' added someone else, until they were all shouting about how well the plan would have worked.

Errol's father glanced over at his son. Errol was sitting quietly in the armchair, stroking Emerald. He was still frustrated with his father for locking up Old Man Ferris, and confused that he had brought him back.

As the children's explanations came to an end, Errol's father commended them on their bravery and daring, and Old Man Ferris stood up. 'Now, children,' he began. 'I have some things I need your help with. Emerald, you too. Follow me!'

They all trooped outside, leaving the room in silence.

Errol's father cleared his throat and moved his chair closer. 'I'm sorry, Errol.' He lifted Swift out of a bag and put the broken pieces on the table. 'I got it wrong. I should never have asked you to give up Swift.'

Errol looked at the broken legs and swallowed.

'I'm not good at repairing things,' his father told him. 'But Old Man Ferris told me he knew someone who could.'

'Who?' Errol whispered.

Errol's father got on his knees in front of his son. 'I think he meant you.' Errol gingerly picked up Swift. It felt as if a great weight had lifted from his shoulders. 'I suppose we could try using some glue from the cupboard.'

Errol's father nodded. Errol found the glue and the two of them sat down at the table to work. They were just finishing when Old Man Ferris appeared at the door.

'Ah, I'm glad you're still here,' he said. 'Errol, your mother wanted to stop by. Is that OK?' Errol nodded. His mother came in and before he knew it she was giving him a big hug. 'I think we should change the rules and appreciate old things as well as new, don't you?' she asked.

'Yes,' said Errol, beaming. 'I do.'

Meanwhile, Old Man Ferris was rummaging around his cupboards and shelves. Eventually he stopped, and tugged his beard.

'If I may be so bold, I have something else that's been restored to its former glory,' he said.

And he held that something out to Errol's father.

Errol's father looked astonished and delighted all

at once. 'My wooden sword!' he exclaimed, taking it from the old man. He looked at Errol. 'My father threw it away when I was a boy because I broke it! That's when the rules began.' He gave the sword a few swings, then showed Errol how to cut, thrust and slice. 'I can't thank you enough,' he said to Old Man Ferris.

The old man bowed. 'A pleasure,' he said. 'And now, would you care to join me outside?' As Errol and his parents stepped out into the night, they gasped. The garden had been transformed. Bunting was hanging in the trees, with lights illuminating

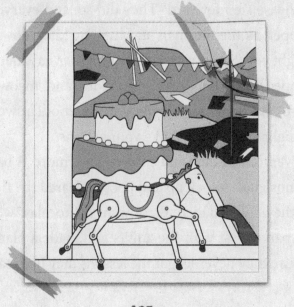

the leaves. Chairs and tables were set out, and all the townspeople were gathered. Piles of misshapen biscuits and cakes sat on the tables with pots of steaming tea.

Errol's parents looked amazed and couldn't stop themselves from cheering along with the crowd.

Then Errol's father motioned for quiet. 'Good citizens,' he said. 'Today I want to honour two people who have shown us all a new way. A way of bringing old things back to life. A way of seeing opportunities rather than rubbish.' He paused, and looked at Old Man Ferris and Errol.

'Please step forward.' They did so, and everyone clapped as the old man and the boy knelt down. 'I knight you, Sir Ferris,' said Errol's father, as Emerald hopped onto Sir Ferris's shoulder and meowed. 'Errol,' his father said, 'I give you my wooden sword. Straight and true, just like your actions.'

Everyone hooted and cheered once more. A band of musicians struck up and people cleared the floor so they could dance. Errol went off to play, while his parents sat with the adults and made a plan to ensure they never forgot the lessons they had learnt that day. Old Man Ferris made another pot of tea, while Emerald sat curled up in an armchair. The party went on into the night, until everyone was so tired they just had to go to bed. Over time, the dusty piles of Junk Town were transformed into new homes, full of old things made good as new. Each one had a lush garden, and Old Man Ferris's home, of course, stood proudly in the centre of them all.

The Leaky Pond

Crash. Sara sat bolt upright in bed and scanned the room, her heart beating fast. Piles of unpacked boxes stood silent as the curtains fluttered in the breeze. And there, over near the window, she saw a broken clay pot and dirt scattered all across the floor.

'Oh no!' she exclaimed. 'That was my favourite flower!'

'Sorry.' *Croak.* 'It was my fault,' said a flat voice from somewhere below her.

Sara yelped and held a pillow in front of her. 'Who's there?' she whispered.

'Me.'

Clutching the pillow tight, Sara plucked up the courage to peer over the edge of the bed.

A dark green lump sat there, with two round eyes staring up. 'I don't jump on demand, if that's what you're thinking.'

'Are you a frog?' she asked. 'I just moved here, and my name is Sara.'

'I am most certainly *not* a frog.' He rolled his eyes. 'Those fancy-prancy-sing-song frogs give the rest of us a bad name.' He sighed. 'If you must know, I'm a toad.'

Sara hesitated. 'Do you want me to kiss you, like in the fairy tales?'

'Yuck!' The toad wiped his thick arm across his lips.

'But that's what it says in the books that Dad reads to me.'

'Well, like you, the books are wrong. Toads don't want kisses.'

Sara propped herself up on her elbows. 'What do you want, then?'

'I need your help,' he mumbled.

'Pardon?' Sara pushed.

'I need your help.' He paused. '*Please.*'

Sara sat up and crossed her legs. 'What do you need help with, Mr Toad?'

'Follow me,' he said, then leapt out into the garden.

She put on her shoes and scrambled over the window ledge. The sun was high in the sky, making her squint.

Croak-croak, rumbled the toad as he hopped down the path.

The garden was wild and overgrown. Sara trailed after Mr Toad until they came to the pond. It was quiet and cool there; a willow tree's branches hung over the water and rustled in the wind. Reeds stood around the banks and lilies covered the surface, hiding its depths; but Mr Toad made his way to the edge and pointed to a dry ring of caked mud.

Sara stared blankly, unsure what the problem was.

The toad tutted. 'The pond is drying up, can't you see?'

'Oh,' Sara replied. 'Well, I guess I can top it up using the garden hose. Would that be OK?'

The toad grinned for the first time as bubbles burst on the surface of the pond. Sara watched as three golden fish came to the surface.

'Hello.' *Pip.*

'Hi.' *Pop.*

'Afternoon.' *Pip*.

'Pleased to meet you,' they said together.

The toad rolled his eyes.

'Reginald! Stop being so grumpy.' The fishes scowled at him.

Sara covered her grin with her hand, trying not to giggle.

'Fine. My name is Reginald and my three friends here are called Philip One, Two and Three. Now, time to top up the water, I think.'

'Pleased to meet you all!' Sara waved to the fishes and then shook Reginald's front leg.

Then she ran to the back of the house, turned on the outside tap and dragged the hose down the garden. Water splattered everywhere, getting her shoes wet and making the ground muddy. Reginald sat, front legs crossed, watching the pond slowly fill up, and the Philips entertained Sara by jumping out of the water and splashing about. Soon the water level was back to normal.

'Thank you, Sara,' said Reginald briskly, and settled himself down near the edge of the pond.

Sara smiled, waved goodbye and went back to her room to bed.

The next day after school, Sara stood inside the swimming pool changing rooms, nervously watching as her new classmates ran off past the showers and towards the water. She pulled her towel tight around her shoulders. It was her first after-school club activity and her dad had insisted it would be OK, but she didn't feel so good. At the poolside, only James, a boy from the class next to hers, hovered at the back like her. Everyone else listened as the instructor explained how they were going to learn some basics.

Sara sidled over. 'James, have you been swimming before?' she whispered.

'No,' he replied, with a shrug.

'Me neither. We didn't have a pool at my last school.'

James looked past her, through the reception area to the games machines. 'I've always been more interested in other stuff. Did you know scientists think crocodiles go back to the same time as dinosaurs? If crocodiles can swim, I reckon dinosaurs could as well.'

Sara half-listened to James, and half-watched the instructor pacing in front of the other children. James was going on and on about how sea serpents, dragons and snakes were all just the same, then how he thought there was a planet out in space with talking dinosaurs.

'You two,' the instructor called sternly. 'At the back. Come forward.'

Sara took a deep breath, just like her dad had taught her, to help control her racing heart. *I wish Dad was here*, she thought. The other children parted as she and James moved to the front. The instructor smiled, but it didn't seem to reach his eyes, and the bright lights above reflected off his shiny bald head.

'I've not seen you before. You're new, I take it?'

Sara felt James breathe a sigh of relief. He'd dodged being picked on. She nodded.

'Right, well, put the towel down and demonstrate what I just explained.'

Sara relived the next few moments all the way home: her foolhardy jump into the pool, then the gasping and kicking until she was pulled out and left to drip on the tiles like a fish out of water. She wanted her whole body to disappear, but it didn't. And to top it off, the instructor made her wear armbands and spend the rest of the lesson in the baby pool while the others practised diving.

As she entered her garden, Sara pictured her dad kneeling down in front of her. 'There is no such thing as failure,' he would say. 'Sometimes just a tough lesson. If you have the courage, you can learn from it.'

He was right. Yes, it had been embarrassing, but there would be an extra lesson tomorrow and she was determined to do better. But how? Who did she know who could help her swim?

As she trotted down to the pond, she had an idea. If anyone could help her, it was Reginald and the Philips! Standing in the same spot as the day before, she bent down and examined the water line. It had gone down again, so she quickly grabbed the garden hose to top it up, all the while looking out for Reginald and the Philips.

'Hello? Hello?' she called.

'What?' Reginald replied from behind some reeds.

'Oh Reggie. Thank goodness you're here!' she grinned, stooping down to greet him.

'I am not *Reggie*. My name is Reginald. Now, what do you want? I am very busy doing nothing, you know.'

'Actually, I was wondering if you could help me,' said Sara.

'Depends. I can help you walk back up the garden. Anything else?'

Disappointed, Sara wasn't sure what to say, so she dabbed at the water's edge with her toe and said nothing. But just then, bubbles broke the water's surface.

'Reginald,' exclaimed Philip One, 'that is no way to treat someone who just topped up the pond without being asked.'

'Hear, hear!' agreed Philip Two.

'How can we help you?' asked Philip Three.

Sara took a deep breath and explained about the swimming lesson. Reginald tutted under his breath and turned away.

'Oh, please don't tut like that!' Sara snapped at him. 'The children at school laughed at me today, and turned away just like that. I thought after yesterday you would be different.'

Reginald's face softened for a moment. He opened his mouth to say something, but the fish beat him to it.

'Of course we'll help!' they cried.

Sara straightened up, starting to feel more

hopeful. 'Thank you!' she said.

'You'll have to make yourself smaller so you can fit in the pond,' Reginald pointed out.

Sara looked confused. 'Smaller? How?'

The toad hopped forward. 'Same as swimming. You *learn*. Now, lie down on the grass and think about being smaller. Think about it so hard that it happens.'

For a moment, Sara thought he was joking. But he didn't seem to be. She could try, couldn't she? Finding a dry spot, she laid down and closed her eyes. Concentrating hard, she pictured herself as small as a dandelion. Her thoughts danced with the wind.

'There you go!' announced Philip One.

'You did it!' shouted Philip Two.

Sara opened her eyes and gasped as she saw the pond stretching out like a lake before her, and Reginald nodding in approval. Only now, he was the same size as her!

'Now wade into the shallow bit,' urged Philip Three, as the other fish lined up the lilies to make swimming lanes.

'First thing you need to do is swish your fins, like this,' Philip One demonstrated.

'Then like this,' Philip Two added.

'Backwards and forwards until you move,' Philip Three instructed.

Sara wiggled her legs and arms like a fish, splashing and coughing.

'No, no, no,' interrupted Reginald. 'She is a human, not a fish! She has legs like a toad, not fins.' He sighed. 'And I thought that dragon was a pain to teach.'

He leapt into the water. 'Like this,' he instructed, as his front legs swept forward in an arc.

Sara tried to copy his movements.

'And sweep out, then bring your arms in. Yes, yes, that's it,' he continued, as Sara followed his example. 'Now move your legs in the same way.' He smiled smugly as Sara began to get the hang of it. 'If you want more speed, you can kick your legs up and down.'

Sara bobbed and then kicked her legs, just like Reginald showed her.

'Perfect. Yes. Very good,' he said. 'Now, swim

up and down those lanes a few times and show yourself how good you are!'

Finally, Reginald settled back on his favourite spot and frowned. 'If you're not swimming like a pro in a couple of weeks, then I'm a frog,' he muttered.

Sara focused on moving her body in the right way. She was clumsy at first, but then she began to enjoy the rhythm and went faster and faster. The Philips swam around her, urging her on and asking her lots of questions. Where was she from? How old was she? Did she like her new home?

Before long, twilight swept across the garden and grey clouds loomed in the distance.

'You did well today,' Reginald piped up, as Sara got out of the water. 'Tomorrow we will start with a new stroke called the butterfly.'

Sara beamed. It took a moment to let her success sink in, and then she lay down by the side of the pond, closed her eyes and imagined herself standing next to it as her normal size. Opening her eyes, she wriggled her toes in the mud and smiled down at her friends.

It was getting chilly now. Wind whipped across the pond, sending shivers down her back. Thanking Reginald and the Philips for their help, Sara went inside for her dinner.

That night, the grey clouds turned into darker clouds and the darker clouds became a storm. Rain poured down, lightning flashed and thunder clapped. In the middle of it all, Sara felt something move at the end of her bed. She rolled back the covers to reveal a shaking green lump.

'Reggie, is that you? What are you doing here?' she asked.

'It's *Reginald*, and I think you should close the window,' he told her.

'But then we wouldn't be able to enjoy the

thunderstorm. Look! See that flash? If we count the seconds until the thunder clap, we can tell how far away the storm is.'

Reginald jumped as the thunder hammered. 'Shut the window so it goes away. Honestly, it's noisier than those silly dancing animals that used to live next to the old pond,' he grumbled.

'Doing that won't make it go away, silly. My mum said that as long as you're inside, thunderstorms can't hurt you. There's nothing to worry about. Come on.' She tiptoed over to the open window. 'Let's watch it!'

Reginald frowned and fidgeted on the spot, then finally hopped over. Settling down next to each other, they watched the big show in the sky.

'Time for bed,' Sara

yawned, as the last of the rain trickled down the window.

'Goodnight,' said Reginald, as he leapt outside. 'And… thanks,' he added, before continuing down the path to his spot.

The next day Sara skipped home from school. Her teacher had been so impressed with her swimming that he had given her a chocolate bar. Leaving her school bag in her bedroom, she scrambled over the window ledge and went down the stony path. Despite yesterday's rain, the pond water had gone down again.

'It's those frogs next door. They're stealing our water for their own pond,' Reginald exclaimed.

Sara scanned the edge of the pond where it met next door's fence. It was like the pond had been cut in half. Curious, she peeked over the fence into the next-door garden, and saw that it had exactly the same design, only the other way round – like an image in a mirror.

'It was one pond once, before humans came along

and plonked a fence across it. The frogs are on that side,' Reginald motioned. 'And the Philips and I are on this side.'

Sara wondered if the frogs were friendly, like the Philips, then absently opened the chocolate wrapper and took a bite. Reginald glanced up and smacked his lips, then quickly crossed his arms and settled into a frown. Sara placed a piece of chocolate in front of him and then disappeared up the path to get the hose. After the pond was topped up again and Reginald had finished his treat, Sara imagined herself small, the way she had before.

'I'm ready to learn, Reggie!' she said, once she'd finished shrinking.

'It's *Reginald*,' he muttered, then puffed out his chest. 'The butterfly stroke.'

As Sara learned how to swing her arms up and around, the Philips leapt out of the water, whooping and shouting. Just as she had the day before, she practised in the lily lanes while Reginald sat and croaked instructions from his spot. Once the lesson had finished, she felt so confident that she rushed out of the pond and gave Reginald a hug.

'Thank you, Reggie!'

He tried to shrink back at first, then couldn't help giving Sara a pat on the back. 'You did well, girl. You did well.'

Finally she waved to the fishes as they swished their fins, imagined herself big and went to have her dinner.

When morning came, Sara threw aside the bed covers and got dressed. *It's the weekend!* she thought. She got out her favourite colouring pencils and a big sheet of paper, and had begun to draw when she heard the window rattle. Dashing over, she pulled it open and looked down.

'It's the Philips. They've been fishnapped!' exclaimed Reginald.

'By who?'

'The frogs! I know it was them. And I still think they've been stealing the pond water as well.'

'But how?' Sara questioned.

'I don't know, but I am going to find out,' declared Reginald.

Sara nodded. 'I'm coming to help you.'

Pulling on her favourite wellies and scrambling out the window, she followed the toad. He led her to a small hole in the fence. Sara pictured herself small and squeezed through the gap. Reginald pushed aside the thick reeds with Sara right behind him. Then, suddenly, he held up his front leg. Sara stopped, and listened.

'Ribbit!'

Sara crouched lower.

'What are you going to do now?' wheezed a wrinkled old frog as he settled on a lily pad.

Three other frogs jumped up and down as the Philips popped up out of the water at the far end of the pond.

'That toad is stealing our water!' they shouted. 'And now we've got his friends, so he'll have to stop!'

The old frog rubbed his forehead. 'You foolish frogs. What good will that do? The Philips were our friends as well before the fence was put up. It was a silly idea.'

'It was not!' the other frogs grumbled.

The Philips swam around the distracted frogs and then bobbed on the surface, trying to get the others' attention. 'Our pond water is going down too,' they said, but the frogs were too busy arguing and complaining about Reginald to listen.

Next to Sara, Reginald puffed his belly in and out. 'Why, I will jump on all of them.'

'Wait, Reggie. Can't you see? The water is going down on this side of the pond as well. There must be a leak. We've got to help!'

Reginald folded his front legs. 'I am not helping frogs.'

'Please, Reggie, for me? And the Philips? They are your friends and they need water in this pond.'

Reginald turned his back and tutted. 'No. I just won't.'

Sara sighed. She would have to act alone for now, and try her best. Pushing back the reeds, she waved and introduced herself to the frogs.

They leapt left and right. 'Ribbit-ribbit. Ribbit-ribbit. What do you want? How did you get here? Who are you?'

Ignoring them, Sara inched nearer to the Philips.

'Sara!' they exclaimed. 'Great to see you. We think we know the problem.'

She nodded slowly. 'Me too.'

As Sara talked to the Philips, the frogs stopped hopping and looked at each other in confusion. Gathering closer, they listened as Sara asked the Philips to check the bottom of the pond for a strong water current, like a little whirlpool.

When the fish disappeared under the water, Sara turned around and faced the frogs.

They puffed out their chests. 'Hey! What are you doing? You can't take the Philips back. We fishnapped them, fair and square.'

Sara put her hands on her hips. 'Once we've checked this side of the pond for leaks, the Philips are coming with me. After all, why would Reggie want to steal your water in the first place? That's a silly idea. He is going to help me find the leak instead. You're welcome to help, if you like.'

The young frogs looked at each other, uncertain. 'You don't know that toad. He is as stubborn as old boots. He won't help you.'

Reginald barged through the reeds. 'You can

insult me and tease me, but never say I won't help my friend!'

Then the old frog slowly hopped forward. 'Forgive them,' he said. 'They still act like tadpoles on their first swim.' Then he turned to Reginald. 'You and I used to be friends before the fence was put up,' he said. 'I shouldn't have let the young ones fishnap the Philips. This girl's courage and willingness to help is a lesson to us all.' He held out a leg. 'Reginald, will you help an old friend who is sorry?'

Sara held back her excitement as Reginald and the old frog shook on it.

Then bubbles popped on the surface of the pond and the Philips appeared.

'I can't see any leaks on the bottom,' Philip One confirmed.

'Not a peep,' Philip Two added.

'Reckon it's on the other side,' Philip Three concluded.

Silence hung in the air. Then Sara saw her chance to lead the group. 'Follow me.'

The frogs shrugged and picked up the Philips. Then they all formed a line and made their way through the reeds and the hole in the fence. Reaching the other side, Reginald invited the old frog to his spot in the reeds, while the Philips and the younger frogs dived into the water to search for the leak.

'We found it!' cheered a frog.

'I said to look there,' chimed in another.

'It was my idea,' complained the last frog.

Sara rolled her eyes. 'Thank you, everyone. So where is the leak?'

'It's where the fence post has been driven into the ground,' exclaimed the Philips.

The frogs exchanged a look and then chorused, 'We found it!'

'About time,' Reginald tutted. 'Now what?'

Sara scratched her head. 'Leave it with me.'

Before long, Sara and her dad were making their way down the garden.

'Look, Dad,' said Sara. 'There's Reggie. Don't call him Reggie, though – he prefers Reginald. And there are the Philips. Say hello to my dad, everyone!'

151

Croak, replied the toad.

Sara frowned. 'I mean, say hello, like you normally do.'

'Croak!' repeated the toad.

Her dad made his way across the reeds to the fence post. 'Pleased to meet you, Mr Reginald. You too, Philip One, Two and Three. Now, let's fix the leak, shall we?'

Sara bent down and whispered to Reginald, 'Why didn't you say hello, Reggie?'

'Because I don't want everyone to know I can talk.' He shifted on the spot and winked. 'It's only meant for special friends.'

Sara grinned, then went to help her dad and the next-door neighbour get everything they needed to repair the leak. First they cleared away the reeds, then put the Philips in buckets of water. Next, her dad wrenched out the fence post and took away the fence. Then all three of them built a new archway and put that where the fence had been.

Finally, when they were all packed up and the sun was beginning to set, Sara let out a contented sigh. The leak was fixed and thanks to the new archway,

the two halves of the pond were joined together to make one again. Fireflies skittered across the water's surface and the frogs ribbited next door.

'I suppose I should properly introduce you to the frogs now,' Reginald piped up.

Sara smiled. 'I suppose you should.'

TImE to Go

Maddie woke with a start. As she stared into the darkness, she gradually worked out that the shadowy shapes across the room were her wardrobe and toy box, and the sound was the blind knocking against the window frame in the breeze. *Just the wind*, she thought.

Then something clattered onto the floor outside her room.

Maddie wrenched the covers over her head and began counting: one, two, three... but it was no good. It was getting hot and what use was a cover against monsters, anyway? *Be brave*, she told herself.

Slowly, she pulled back the cover and slipped out of bed. She grabbed her pillow and held it up, ready to strike, then crept across the room. No one was going to scare her any more.

In the dark hallway, her great grandpa's old wooden toy horse wobbled mid-air next to the side table, then fell. Maddie winced, but the crash never happened. Instead the horse floated back to its original place, and Maddie could just make out the name *Swift* written on its belly.

'Phew,' someone gasped.

The floorboards creaked under Maddie's feet. Suddenly a glittering dark cloud shot out from under the table, picked up a photo of her parents, then swished down the stairs.

Maddie rushed over, gripped the banister and watched the strange cloud disappear towards the kitchen. Curiosity tugged her down the steps, one at a time. She knew she should get her parents, but her mum was sick and she didn't want to disturb her dad after his long working day.

The lid of the largest saucepan on the hob rattled shut as Maddie tiptoed onto the cold kitchen floor. The fridge hummed in the corner. The clock on the oven read 01:32, the numbers glowing blue.

'I'll have to get ready for school in six hours,'

Maddie moaned to herself, but her routine was quickly forgotten when the saucepan lid rattled again.

Mrs Jenkins the cat looked down from her perch on top of the fridge, staring wide-eyed at the hob.

Maddie poked the saucepan with her pillow. 'I know you're in there. Now come out and give the photograph back.'

Nothing happened.

'Come on, or I'll push you off.'

The lid lifted a little. Maddie frowned and peeped around the pillow. The lid lifted a little more and glittering dark liquid flowed over the side, pooling on the hob. The photo frame was nowhere to be seen.

'So, where's the photograph?' Maddie demanded.

The liquid reached back inside the saucepan, fished out the picture, and placed it in Maddie's open hand.

'Good. Thank you,' she said. 'Now, who are you and what are you doing in my house?'

Part of the liquid formed a mouth. 'My name is . . . Groblet,' the mouth whispered. 'But you're not supposed to see me.'

'I *can* see you, though!' Maddie exclaimed.

'I know.' Groblet started gliding back and forth across the hob. 'My boss didn't prepare me for this. "Don't worry, they won't see you" that's what he said. Now what do I do? I'm only an assistant. This is the last time I offer to stand in. It's a big responsibility. Can't you go away?' he asked Maddie finally. 'We can pretend this never happened. Yes. That's a good idea.'

Maddie tilted her head to the side, confused and interested all at once. 'Groblet . . . what *are* you?'

'I'm a Transcendental Hyperaware Interdimensional Numinous Guide – or *thing*, for short.'

Maddie frowned. A *what*?

'I guess you would call me a spirit, though that's not very accurate,' Groblet added.

'Oooh, like a ghost? Dad always pretends to be a ghost at Halloween. Are you supposed to be in a white sheet and say booooo?'

'No,' Groblet replied flatly. 'I'm a guide. We do *not* scare people.'

Maddie crossed her arms. 'So who are you guiding and where are they going?'

Groblet stopped sliding and faced her. 'We guide those whose turn it is to pass from this place to the next. That's how my boss describes it. Some run down the road headlong, others need a hand, he'd say. I can understand that. It's hard to let go, if only for a moment, and easy to get lost. Either way, my instruction is to greet them, walk alongside them, and listen to their stories. As for where . . .' Groblet twisted towards the window. 'It's like the path beyond your garden gate. You can't see it, but you know it's there. Like the next train station down the line.'

Maddie's heartbeat quickened as she realised what Groblet meant. 'You mean . . . when people die, don't you?'

The glittering liquid slowly nodded.

Maddie thought hard. She remembered the moment when Dad had knelt down in front of her and explained her mum's illness. Dread had filled the pit of her stomach.

'Maddie darling,' her dad had said. 'You know when Mr Jenkins wasn't very well? We had to go to the vet and say goodbye. Remember how sad we felt? Well, Mummy is sick like that. She is with the special doctors now. She has asked to see you. Will you come with me?'

Maddie had agreed, but nothing had prepared her for seeing her mum like that, lying there so pale. All the tubes, beeps and white blankets. The sharp, unnatural smell. Mum had come home a week later, but she couldn't get out of bed.

Maddie hadn't cried since that day, but now she could feel the tears bubbling up. 'Your boss… he's Death, isn't he? And my mum . . . she's your guest?'

Groblet became a glittering cloud again and started drifting over her head. 'Yes,' he said, in a softer tone.

'Wait! You can't! Stop! Not yet…' Maddie replied. She wasn't ready to say goodbye. She shouldn't have to let go.

'It's been the way of things since long before you

and I came along. Beginning and endings. Hellos and goodbyes. I'm sorry, but I really must go now.'

But then, all of a sudden, Mrs Jenkins the cat leapt off the fridge and swiped a paw through the glittering cloud.

Achoo 'Oh no!' A puff of sparkles spread across the kitchen top. 'I'm allergic to cats.' *Achoo!*

Maddie took her chance, rushed across the room and shut the door. The glittering cloud swirled above her, while Mrs Jenkins began washing herself with her paw.

Maddie's mind raced. There must be a way around it. If only there was a way to get more time to think. 'Please. Mum always said she had so much left to tell me. She made a promise. She won't be able to leave with a broken promise. There must be a way you can help.'

Groblet settled into a blob again, on the kitchen floor as far away from Mrs Jenkins as possible. 'It's dangerous playing with time, but there is something we could do. We could visit your mum in the past. You'd get to see her, but you couldn't let her know it's you. We would still have to come back here afterwards, and it might not be as you imagined. I don't know. It's too risky. I shouldn't have said anything...'

'Please,' Maddie interrupted.

Groblet glided over to where she stood. 'All right then. Hold out the photograph and close your eyes.'

'This?' Maddie asked, looking down at the photo.

'Yes. Photos are like windows to the past. Now close your eyes and think of your mum in that picture. Repeat after me: *time to go*.'

Maddie squeezed her eyes shut and whispered the words . . .

Bright sunshine beat down. Maddie felt the heat warming her bare arms instantly. She could hear the sound of cars whizzing down the road behind her and feel the soft grass under her feet. As she slowly opened her eyes, she could hear the familiar voices of her mum and dad.

'Hold that pose. You look great!' said her dad, looking at his camera.

'Do I? I feel like a whale with this baby inside me.'

Joy blossomed inside Maddie. Her parents were full of life, just how she remembered before Mum got sick. She continued watching while they took more photos and got out a picnic. Then all of a sudden her dad took out his phone and read a message, then hugged her mum and jogged off.

A black cat appeared from behind the nearest tree and began rubbing itself against Maddie's leg.

'Is that you, Groblet? I didn't know you could become a cat,' Maddie whispered.

Groblet looked up and winked. 'Now you know.'

'I thought you didn't like cats.'

'I'm allergic. That doesn't mean I don't like them. Besides, being one is very different.'

Maddie looked at her mum again. She wanted to run over, but Groblet's warning held her back.

'Can we say hello?'

Groblet didn't reply. Instead, he trotted over to where the picnic lay spread out. Maddie ran after him and stood there with her hands clasped in front of her.

'Hi,' she announced.

'Hello there,' her mum replied. 'That's a nice cat. Are you lost? Where are your parents?'

'Thanks. I'm not lost. They're in the park.' Maddie turned and pointed over to the swings and slide.

'Oh. What's your name then? Mine is Sara,' said her mum.

'My name is Maddie.'

'That's funny. I'm going to name my baby Madeline. Pleased to meet you. Would you like some sandwiches? My husband had to go, and all this food needs eating.'

'No, thank you.'

Sara smiled. 'All right.' She rummaged in her bag and pulled out a small story book. 'What do you think of this present I got for my little girl? She isn't born yet, but hopefully she'll like it.'

'You know it was my favourite,' Maddie replied quickly, without thinking.

At that, Groblet meowed loudly.

'He's lively, isn't he?' Sara stroked his head. 'Did your mum read this story to you as well? I thought it had only been published recently.'

A lump rose in Maddie's throat. 'Yes.'

Then her mum glanced into her bag and tutted. 'Oh no! My husband's wallet. He'll need this. I'd better call him. Excuse me for a second.'

She got out her phone and dialled a number. Maddie picked up the book and flipped through the pages, letting her mum's voice fade into comforting background noise. When the call ended, Sara announced that she needed to leave to go and meet her husband. Maddie remained silent and thought of all the things they could do, like go on the swings or play hide and seek, but in a flash the picnic was packed away, and Sara was standing up.

'Please don't go,' Maddie started, but then corrected herself. 'I mean, you need to finish your sandwich, don't you?'

Groblet jumped up, trying to stop Maddie from keeping her mother there, but she pushed the cat away.

Sara narrowed her eyes for a second, then smiled. 'Why do I feel like I know you?'

'You don't.' Maddie blushed. 'I promise.'

Sara shook her head, then turned towards the park gate. 'Lovely to meet you, Maddie. Enjoy the sunshine.'

As her mum disappeared around the corner, Maddie automatically stepped forward, but Groblet stood in her way.

'It's time to go, don't you think?' he pointed out gently.

'No, I want to go with her. Why can't I? You can't stop me.' Maddie stamped her foot.

Groblet sat on his haunches and just stared at her.

'It's not fair, Groblet. I don't want to say goodbye. She's my mum. It's not fair.'

Just then, a piece of paper skittered across the grass on the breeze and came to rest on her shin. Maddie reached down to pick it up.

'Oh look, Groblet.' She held it out, her frustration melting away. 'It's my dad's favourite picture of my mum. He said it was taken right before their first date. It must have fallen out of his wallet. She looks so beautiful.'

Groblet's tail swished.

'I could run and give it back to her, couldn't I?' Maddie suggested. 'Otherwise, how would I know about it?'

'I don't think that's a good idea. Besides, things like that have a way of returning to their rightful place,' said Groblet, looking up at Maddie's desperate face. Then he hesitated. 'I suppose we could do what we did before with that photo.'

'Can we?' Maddie grinned.

'Come on then,' Groblet agreed, reluctantly. 'Say the words after me.'

Maddie opened her eyes. 'Groblet, where are you?'

A hamster poked its head out of the pocket on her top. 'I'm here, of course.'

Maddie looked around. They appeared to be in a changing room with a big mirror. *Where are we?* she wondered, drawing back the thick blue curtain. The shop assistant nodded as Maddie peered past her into the main part of the shop. Racks of clothes were everywhere: all different shapes, colours and styles. Unfamiliar music blared out from the speakers overhead. Lots of older girls milled around, picking out items and putting them back. Maddie didn't recognise the shop's name, but knew she was in the women's section.

Groblet poked his head out again. 'There are a lot of people here. Haven't they got anything better to do? I can't see your mum anywhere, either.' He scrambled onto her shoulder and looked around. 'Who's making that noise?'

Maddie turned and listened. Someone was talking to themselves really loudly in one of the cubicles, complaining about some clothes. The shop assistant looked nervous. Something told Maddie she should go and see what was going on. She cleared her throat and shook the curtain a little.

'Hello. My name is Maddie. Can I help you?'

'Hmmph. Come in.'

Maddie pulled back the curtain. Her mum stood there with a frown, holding up a pale blue dress. She was much younger than before. There were no lines on her forehead and her hair was shorter. Other dresses were hanging on the hooks and the small bench of the changing room.

'Sorry. I must be making a racket. I just can't find the right dress and my date is in half an hour. What am I going to do?'

'I'm sure I can help!' Maddie replied without a second thought, ignoring Groblet fidgeting in her pocket.

'Can you? I'm so stuck. I don't want to look frumpy. This guy is so handsome! My name is Sara, by the way. I like Maddie. Short for Madeline, right? What do you think of this pale blue?'

Maddie blinked for a moment, trying to take it all

in. 'It makes you look a bit frumpy.'

'That's what I thought.' Sara covered her face with her hands. Maddie picked up a yellow dress from the bench. 'What about this one instead?'

'I don't like it. The sleeves are too long and it makes me look too pale.'

Groblet poked his head out and whispered, 'Black is always a safe bet.'

Maddie scanned the cubicle, but none of the clothes were black. Without a word, she went and asked for help.

A few moments later, an assistant came back with an armful of other items. 'Here are the dresses for your sister.'

'She isn't my sister, but thank you,' Maddie replied.

The shop assistant raised her eyebrows, then put the dresses with the others on the bench.

'She's got a point, you know. We do look alike,' Sara mused.

After trying on six more, they finally found the right dress, a long-sleeved one with a star pattern that stopped at the knee. Sara handed the rest back to the assistant.

As they walked through the shop and over to the cashier, Sara chatted away to Maddie. 'I'm using the birthday money my mum gave me. I really hope he likes it! I wonder what he'll be wearing. We're going to that nice Italian place across town. Can you hold this for me? It's a card my mum sent me.'

Sara handed the card to Maddie while she paid. It had bouncing rabbits, foxes doing the foxtrot and a troll stretched out in a dance pose with a big grin – all under bunting that spelt out 'Happy Birthday'. *What a funny card*, Maddie thought.

Soon they were standing by the shop door, looking out at pouring rain.

'Will you take a photo of me?' Sara asked. 'Then at least I'll have evidence that I looked good before the rain.'

Maddie nodded, and used her mum's old camera to take the photo her dad would treasure.

'Thank you for helping me,' said Sara. 'I've got to go now. Wish me luck!'

'Good luck,' Maddie replied, then waved as her mum dashed down the street.

As soon as she was out of sight, Maddie felt that

empty dull ache come back. She looked down and realised she was still holding the birthday card.

'Wait! You forgot this!' she shouted.

But her mum had disappeared. Groblet squeaked in protest.

'I know. We shouldn't go after her,' Maddie grumbled.

'No, we shouldn't.'

Maddie opened the card and a small black and white photo fell out. She picked it up. It was a portrait of her mum at about the same age that Maddie was now. It read:

Dear Sara,
Happy birthday darling. Get something nice! This photo is of you at school when you were ten. How time flies.
Love you lots, Mum.

'Can we use the photo again? Please, Groblet. We're so alike, Mum and I.'

'We really shouldn't.'

'Just once more?'

'*Just once more?*' Groblet repeated. 'How many *just once mores* are we going to have? This isn't a game, you know.'

'I know,' Maddie replied quietly.

Groblet crawled up onto her shoulder and let out a little sigh. 'Well, I guess I'm in trouble already, so we probably can't make it much worse. OK then. This is the last time, though.'

Maddie picked up the hamster and held him close. 'Oh, thank you, Groblet.'

'Yes. Yes. Enough of that. Hold the picture and say the words after me.'

'Time to go,' Maddie said, with gusto.

She opened her eyes and found herself in a school classroom.

'Who are you?' said a girl who looked just like Maddie. 'I've not seen you in school before. Have you just started?'

'Mmm. Yes. My parents are with the headmaster. My name is Maddie.'

'Mine's Sara. What's the name of your puppy? Is he a black Labrador? Didn't know we were allowed to bring pets to school.'

Maddie glanced down. 'Oh, er… yes, he is. His name's Groblet. I'm looking after him for my parents. What are you doing?'

Sara sighed. 'Nine times table. Though I'd rather play with your puppy.'

'I've just learned that. My mum taught me a great way to do it.' Maddie walked over to Sara's little desk. 'See, look at the first number of the answer. It goes up one at a time. Two times nine is eighteen. The first number is one. Three times nine is twenty-seven. The first number is two. Four times nine is thirty-six. The first number is three. Can you guess the first number of five times nine?'

'Four?' Sara replied.

'Yes. Now we know the first number goes up one at a time. The second number is always what you need to add to the first number to make nine. So if two times nine is eighteen, and we know the first number is one, then the second number must be eight because then it makes nine. It's the same for three times nine. The first number is two, so the second number must be seven because that makes nine, and the answer is twenty-seven – two and seven. If the first number for five times nine is four, like you said, what's the second number?'

Sara tapped her fingers on the paper as she counted. 'Five? So the answer to five times nine is forty-five and then the answer to six times nine is a five and a four, so fifty-four?'

'Yes!' Maddie grinned.

With Maddie helping, they'd soon finished all Sara's work, so they chased Groblet around the room until they heard a voice from the corridor.

'Sara! Finish what you're doing and come along for the school photos!'

'I've got to go,' said Sara. 'That's Mrs Windthrup, my teacher. Guess I'll see you around?'

Maddie bit her lip. 'I'm not sure. We're visiting lots of schools...'

Sara nodded and left. The door shut slowly behind her.

Groblet didn't say anything as Maddie stood for a moment. 'I know, Groblet. It's time to go.' A stray tear ran down her cheek.

Groblet transformed into the glittery cloud that Maddie had first met, and settled around her shoulders.

'You're warm,' Maddie realised absently, as Groblet pulled himself a little tighter. 'How do we get back?'

'Don't worry, I know a way. You can use mirrors and even some doors. We can use that mirror over here.' Groblet floated over to one hanging on the wall. 'Close your eyes and step through with me.'

Maddie's heart sank as she recognised the buzz of the fridge. They were back in the kitchen. The clock on the oven read 01:40. There was no turning back now.

'Was it real, Groblet?'

'As real as you or I.'

Groblet floated over to the closed door. Mrs Jenkins the cat dropped onto the floor and joined him. Maddie couldn't hold back the tears any more as she slowly crossed the kitchen and made her way with Groblet and Mrs Jenkins up the stairs. Pausing at the hallway table, she placed the photo of her mum back in its place. Then she touched her Grandpa's wooden horse. It always reminded her of his stories from faraway lands.

'Can I come in, too?' she asked.

'Of course,' said Groblet softly. 'Why don't you hold her hand?'

Quietly, they entered her parents' room. Her mum was lying on her back, face relaxed, an arm folded across her chest. Her dad faced the opposite wall, snoring. Maddie tried to swallow the lump in her throat as she knelt and held her mum's hand.

'Time to go, Mum. Don't worry, Groblet will be with you.'

There was no bright light when her mum left, only a whisper on the breeze that said, 'Follow me.' Maddie's dad woke up, and together, through the tears, they said goodbye.

Something changed inside Maddie after that night. She didn't feel angry or desperate any more. She just missed her mum, like we all miss the ones we love when they're not with us the way they used to be.

Many nights later, when she was holding a photo of her mum and thinking about her time with Groblet, she heard a knock on her mirror.

'Hello?'

'Hello.' Groblet swirled into the centre of the room. 'Your mum sends her love. She remembers meeting you all those times now.'

'Oh.' Maddie looked down at the photo.

'She misses you as well, you know. Now, tell me what you've been up to at school,' said Groblet, and together they started a different type of journey.

Insider Spider

Herbert the Third launched through the gap in the sash window, using four of his eight hairy legs to vault the rest of his body over the high lip of the ledge. Being a spider had its advantages, and strength was one of them! Behind him, outside on the flower box, the wind whistled through a threadbare web covered with raindrops. He sighed as he looked back at it. It was his first attempt at a web, and nothing like his parents' place. *The Webbertons take pride in building their webs inside*, they used to say, so here he was – finally inside, trying to follow in their footsteps. This was a different house, of course, but his fangs had grown and he had hair on his skinny legs, just like his sisters and brothers who'd left home before him.

He wondered how the other Herberts were getting along. *Don't settle for a cave or a shed, dears. Nowhere too hot or too cold, either*, his mother used to warn them all when they were growing up.

I hope they've found a nice spot like the inside of this window, thought Herbert as he examined the potential of his new pad. The room was huge in comparison to the ledge outside. Grey early morning light cast shadows across the towering wood and fabric surfaces. *They call it furniture, dear*, his mother had explained to him. *Those big things – humans – they sit on it all the time. No fly-catching for them! They don't like it when they see you on their furniture, so avoid it. You can hide under the big long ones if you're in a pinch, though.*

He decided to stay where he was. Next to him, tucked in the corner, stood a small crystal ball, like the ones used by fortune tellers. When he got closer, he noticed his reflection stretch wider and wider.

He grinned, letting each of his fangs show, and raised his eyebrows. 'Well hello there, Herbert the Third, best of his name.'

After exploring the rest of the window sill he

stood up and put four of his legs on his hips. *This place looks as good as any*, he convinced himself, and began stringing his fine threads from some of the corners. After spinning the basic layout, he heard something creak behind him. To his surprise, a human rushed into the room, its footsteps booming across the wooden floor.

Oh, bother, Herbert thought. *I was rather hoping not to have to deal with them while I was setting up.*

A bright light flared up in a large globe up above. Herbert covered his eyes, then looked down.

Oh no! His dark body was now highlighted by the white shiny surface of the window. This wasn't going at all how he'd planned.

'Can't you go back to the other room?' the spider grumbled out loud to the human walking around.

His heart pumped as he remembered his mother's warning. *Now, Herberts, they might be big, but they scare easily. In fact, they'll trap you under a see-through prison, shove something under your feet and then throw you out of the window. It's not nice, especially in winter. It's best to run and hide somewhere until they give up. You might lose your web, but at least you can build another one.*

So, Herbert scrambled over to a corner, hoping the shadows would conceal him. But just as he was making a dash for it, the wind rattled the window frame, drawing the attention of the human.

'Arrrghhh . . . a spider!' The shriek echoed across the room, then the human disappeared for a moment before returning holding a piece of paper and a see-through thing.

Herbert quickly held up one of his front legs in protest. 'N-n-no. Wait! Please stop. It's a long way down if you throw me out of the window. I won't do anything bad, I promise.'

The human's forehead wrinkled in surprise as he held the see-through prison suspended in the air above Herbert. 'Eh? I could swear I just heard you talking . . . I must be tired.'

Herbert covered his mouth as the human's hot breath washed over him. *What do humans eat to make them smell so bad?*

Knowing there was no escape off the window sill, Herbert gave up and scuttled forward. The prison came over his head and cut off all the sound, then he had to jump up as the paper shot under his feet. Suddenly the world turned upside down and he saw the window being opened wider. *I knew I should have just let the wind batter me and the rain soak my web*, he concluded. Hovering outside in the glass prison, Herbert tried to hold on as the paper was pulled away, but there was nothing to grip onto, so he sailed down to the bushes like a raindrop.

☆☆☆

It took Herbert all day to crawl back up to his original web on the flower box outside the window, and by the time he got there, it was dark. *One day*, he thought as he looked inside, *one day, someone will understand that I'm not a monster.* Just then, a flash of light shot up into the sky from the house across the road. It shimmered with all of the colours of the rainbow, then stopped, leaving just the orange glow of the street lights. *I wonder what's in that house,* thought Herbert. He rubbed his front legs together, and grinned.

The Zogs and the Alien

James held on to his telescope tightly as he squinted with one eye up at the clear, dark night sky. He twiddled the focus setting on the side to try to get a better view of the brightest stars, just as his grandad had shown him. This week at school he had been taught that all the stars were just like the sun, except very far away, with planets orbiting them as well. He looked up again. There were so many, which meant there had to be trillions and zillions of planets – not that James could see them, even with the telescope. *Just because you don't see them doesn't mean they're not there*, his teacher had pointed out. That had left James thinking about the endless possibilities: planets with dragons, planets with ice-cream mountains and furry aliens that said *yipper* to everything. The more he learned, the more it proved his secret theory: that magic and science were one and the same thing – just different points of view.

The wind sent a shiver up his legs. It was getting late and he was already supposed to be in bed. He folded up the tripod and lowered it onto his bedroom floor, then hopped through the window. Gravelly bits from the flat roof outside his bedroom were stuck between his toes, so he began to brush them off. But just then a tennis ball rolled across the floor, and something rustled near his chest of drawers.

James stopped what he was doing. 'Hey! Who's there?'

Nothing stirred.

Then someone muttered, 'We should say something to the Earthling.'

It was a weird voice, James thought – just like his mum's talking clock.

'I agree,' replied another robotic voice.

'Shhh. I say we shouldn't!' someone else grumbled in a crotchety tone.

James listened intently, grabbing his pillow just in case he needed to thwack one of them.

'I am the leader and I say we should!' continued the grumpy one.

'But you just said we shouldn't!'

'I did not. I was thinking out loud.'

'I agree.'

'Who agrees?'

'Be quiet. I will speak now.'

James's mouth dropped open as the room filled with a warm, bright orange light. Three large egg-shaped creatures focused their eyes on him. The one on the left was glowing purple, the one in the middle was a gleaming green, and the one on the right was bright orange. Each sat on a cushioned metal platform with two arms extending out. A set of wheels drove the green one forward.

'Greetings, Earthling!'

James squinted in the light. 'You're aliens!'

The trio glanced at each other. 'Incorrect, Earthling. We are Zogs. *You* are the alien.'

James looked down at himself for a second in confusion.

'You will come with us!' insisted the green Zog.

Excitement flooded through James. Real aliens – or Zogs, or whatever they were – were going to abduct him! But then he had a thought.

'I can't,' he said. 'I've got school in the morning and my mum would go bananas.'

The trio rotated their platforms and went into a huddle. As they continued to wobble and whisper, he grabbed some socks from the floor.

Then the trio rotated towards him. 'I am the leader, Captain Zog. You will be returned before school. Now you will come with us,' commanded the green Zog.

Thoughts raced around James's head. Should he go? He looked up at the posters on his wall – a rocket blasting off; a picture of his favourite film character, an artificial intelligence cat; and the solar system.

Surely it would be just like a field trip? James thought. *And more proof for my theory that there could be all sorts of creatures living out in space.* He looked at the Zogs again. True, these aliens weren't quite what he'd expected, but then, what had he expected? There were endless possibilities, after all. *My friends will think I am crazy. Or really cool!* He thought.

That was it. He'd made his decision. He nodded at the trio, and put on his socks and trainers. Then he shoved his pillow under the bedcovers to make it look like he was there, and sleeping.

'Where are we going?' he asked.

'Back to our ship, where you will be transported across the galaxy to another planet called Zog!'

The trio wheeled closer.

'Hang on, I don't even know your names.'

'I've told you. We are the Zogs!'

They formed a circle around him, and suddenly James was whooshing upwards through a kaleidoscope of colour, passing through his bedroom ceiling like torchlight into the night. Clouds whizzed by on a rollercoaster ride through the atmosphere. He could see the Zogs in front of him with their wheels tucked underneath their platforms. Then, in the distance, he saw an oval shape that grew bigger and bigger. *It must be the spaceship!* he thought. It didn't seem possible to

go any faster,
but all the same,
they sped up as
they hurtled
towards it. *Surely
we should be slowing
down, like Dad when
he parks the car*, James
thought, his heart racing.

And then a hatch opened
and James catapulted through
it, crashing straight into a thick band. The hatch
clanked shut as he hung there, arms over it, limp
like wet clothes on a washing line.

'What a ride!' he gasped.

Catching his breath, James took in his surroundings. The room was bright yellow and
padded all over, like a bouncy castle. The Zogs
hovered on the spot, looking at him. On the floor,
a bundle of blankets caught his attention. It was
moving gently up and down as though someone
was sleeping under it. *I wonder who that is?* he
thought.

'Captain Zog to the bridge,' echoed an announcement, as a doorway whooshed open.

'Stay here, Earthling,' Captain Zog commanded.

James lifted his arms off the band and put his hands on his hips. 'Hey, that's not fair. I want to see us going at lightspeed as we travel to Zog!'

Captain Zog narrowed his eyes and kept silent. The other two Zogs carried on hovering quietly either side of James.

'Do not worry, Earthling, the captain is a grumpy Zog,' comforted the purple Zog.

'My name is James, not Earthling,' James snapped.

'Greetings, James,' replied the orange Zog.

The boy looked at the pair and back at the captain. 'What will we do when we get to your planet?'

'You are here to defeat the red Zog for me. I am not allowed. I am a captain,' said the green Zog.

James felt butterflies in his stomach. *Maybe I should have stayed at home*, he thought. Then again, this could be pretty exciting.

The blanket stirred. A man stood up, folded the

cover and placed it back on the floor. 'We be here to compete in a game, lad,' he informed James in a grizzly voice.

The man was wearing a baggy white shirt, big brown boots and an eye patch. His ginger beard was thick and curly, like the hair on his head. He was cradling a small animal that was furry all over, with big ears, long legs and a long tail – a bit like a rabbit, but bigger.

'The game is of the intergalactic sort, with a great number of ladders and some devilishly tricky snakes. Being eaten was a possibility mentioned to me, but the good Zogs reassure me it doesn't happen often.' The man strode over and offered his hand. 'I be a pirate and this here is Joey – he's a baby kangaroo.'

James tried to take it all in. He shook the pirate's hand. 'You're really a pirate? Holding a kangaroo! In a spaceship? With three aliens?' He looked at the captain. 'And you want me to compete against a red Zog in an inter-something game of Snakes and Ladders?'

The pirate looked at the Zogs, pursed his

lips, then raised an eyebrow. 'That be a good summary!' He nodded.

'This is why you were chosen,' added the Zogs in unison.

Chosen? James thought, but before he had a chance to ask any more questions, another announcement boomed across the room. 'Everyone prepare for space jump.'

The ship's engines started, making the room vibrate, and the Zogs left.

'Welcome aboard, lad!' the pirate said, grabbing the blanket and tying it around his shoulders. 'You're about to feel like a fish in a stormy sea.'

James frowned. The ship's hum grew louder, making him feel lightheaded. 'Mr Pirate,' he called out. 'What's happening? I feel funny.' He tried to blink away the dizziness as the room started to whirl.

'Aye, it's a pirate's life,' the man replied, and cartwheeled through the air.

James glanced at the pirate, then at his own hands, and suddenly realised what was happening. 'I'm floating!' he exclaimed.

After enjoying a few twists and tumbles, James heard the ship's hum abruptly stop, and they landed back on the floor with an *umph*. James heard the whoosh of the door and sat up, while the pirate rolled over and began to snore.

'Earthlings! Welcome to planet Zog,' a Zog greeted them.

The curved ceiling of the spaceship wobbled like a jelly and then melted away. James shielded his eyes as bright lights appeared, then peered this way and that to see what lay beyond them. He soon realised that the ship was in the middle of a massive round stadium. Zogs of all shapes and sizes were in the seats that rose up on all sides around them. James felt his palms grow sweaty. He didn't know whether to feel excited or terrified. He'd only ever seen this many spectators when he was watching sport with his family! He patted himself down. *Yep, I'm here – it's not a dream*, he thought, then took a deep breath. The crowd exploded with cheers as he stepped forward.

'So where's the Snakes and Ladders board, Captain Zog?' he asked.

To his surprise, his voice echoed around the stadium, and the crowd roared again.

'Er . . . hello, everyone?' he said, just to make sure he wasn't imagining things.

Thousands of Zogs shouted, 'Hello, Earthling!'

Caught up in the moment, James spoke again. 'Hello, planet Zog! Let's play some Snakes and Ladders!'

Now the crowd started to chant. 'Snakes and Ladders, Snakes and Ladders!'

James dashed over to the pirate. Even over the noise, he could still hear him snoring. 'Wake up. Wake up!' he urged. 'We're about to start playing!'

As the pirate sat up and rubbed his eyes, the ground shook. A new structure began to rise up next to the spaceship, and then grew taller and taller. It was made of cubes, like lots of box rooms stacked on top of each other, and only stopped growing once it was ten cubes high and ten across. Each cube shone like polished glass in the bright lights. As the crowd quietened, the stadium lights dimmed and everywhere became dark. Everything seemed to pause. It was tense. Numbers flashed rapidly on the cubes in alternating colours and from left to right – one, two, three, all the way up to one hundred. Doors opened at different points between

the cubes as ladders appeared from the ground, and massive snakes slithered into place. The audience went wild.

James gulped as he watched the snakes open and close their gaping jaws.

'Don't worry, lad,' said the pirate, patting his shoulder.

An announcement introduced the contestants one by one. First there was a large, red, scowling Zog, then a tiny blue one who hopped when the spotlight was on him. Then it was James's turn, and finally the pirate's, with his kangaroo.

Once they'd been introduced, the four contestants were escorted to cube number one, and each given dice. As the rules were read out, James glanced across at the red Zog; lumps like blisters appeared down his sides in strips, making him look meaner than ever.

'The green Zogs have opted to have two non-Zog champions play on their behalf instead of one Zog, the Earthlings. Should our galactic guests lose the contest,' the voiceover went on to warn, 'the green Zog captain will forfeit ownership of the green spaceship to the red Zogs, who have entered one of their own champions. In the spirit of fairness, the blue Zogs have also been allowed to participate.'

James's mind reeled. If neither he nor the pirate won, the green Zog captain wouldn't control the spaceship – so how would he get home? The red Zog didn't look like he would help. James would be stuck on planet Zog. He'd never get to eat pizza or watch AI Cat again, or prove that space worms made wormholes. *No*, he steeled himself. *I'm an explorer. Now is not the time to panic.* He had to win.

He focused on the voiceover. 'If the competing red Zogs lose, their captain has to give up the time-warp cruiser to the green Zogs. Should the blue Zogs win, they will get to choose one or the other.'

For the first time, James noticed another particularly wrinkly red Zog standing outside. *That must be the equivalent captain for the red Zogs*, he thought.

Everyone cheered one last time, and the game started. The large red Zog rolled first and got a six. Lights flashed neon blue as the commentator announced a bonus roll. That produced a three, so the large Zog bundled through the whooshing doors to cube nine – then hopped straight up a ladder to cube thirty-one. The muted roar of the crowd barely penetrated the plastic cubes as all the red Zogs cheered their champion.

'Luck of the dice,' said the pirate.

'I hope I'm lucky then,' commented the small blue Zog.

'Me too,' agreed James.

The blue Zog rolled a four and ascended a ladder up to cube fourteen, much to the delight of his followers.

Then James heard a small voice in his ear telling him it was his turn. He took a deep breath and let the dice fall onto the floor. *For the pizza!* he encouraged himself. The dice bounced and bounced, finally landing on a six. *Yes!* he thought. He quickly picked it up and rolled again. He got a two and let out a sigh. He walked to cube eight and looked out at Captain Zog near the spaceship. The captain raised an eyebrow and jerked his egg-shaped head, as if to say, 'Hurry up and win!'

Next, the pirate rolled a four and went up a

ladder to cube fourteen to join the blue Zog. James gave him a thumbs-up. *As long as one of us beats the Zogs*, he thought, as he looked at everyone above him.

Two rounds later and the pirate celebrated taking the lead by dancing a jig in cube forty-two. The red Zog fumed as he went into second place. The blue Zog remained in third, leaving James in last place. Nagging doubts began to creep up on him. What if he lost? *Nothing I can do about it now*, he tried to tell himself calmly. *I need to focus.*

A round later and James was slowly making progress; he'd reached cube twenty-two on the third level. He looked up as the blue Zog climbed the ladder from twenty-eight to eighty-four, taking the lead from the pirate, who was in cube forty-eight. The red Zog seemed to be getting redder and redder after each low number he rolled.

The blue Zog rolled a one, and then it was James's turn. His luck was clearly running out, because he only managed a one as well. He had got into the habit of glancing out at Captain Zog, and what he saw didn't make him feel very good about still being last. The captain was looking at the ground, wobbling from side to side. Thoughts of playing games at home popped into James's head: *it was so easy back there*. He took a step forward into cube twenty-five.

The pirate fared better and rolled a three, leaping up a ladder to cube sixty-seven as the crowd cheered the new underdog. Then, out of nowhere the red Zog rolled a six and then another six and then a five. As he stormed through the whooshing doors, the crowd waited with bated breath. He was heading straight for a cube with a snake's head in it. He barged through the last doorway and bellowed at the top of his voice. The shocked snake retreated, and the red Zog stayed still.

James waited for someone to intervene, but nothing happened.

'He's cheating!' he shouted. 'Slide down the snake to thirty-four, you cheat!'

The crowd booed and the snakes hissed. The red Zog's flat mouth twitched, but he stayed exactly where he was.

James gasped in dismay at the red Zog's behaviour.

Then the blue Zog shrugged and rolled a three. He hopped onto a long snake's body and slid down to twenty-four. The pirate gave a thumbs-up as James rolled a three and went up to cube eighty-four.

'Yeah!' shouted James, jumping up and down, and Captain Zog beamed with satisfaction.

Then the pirate got a four and went from sixty-seven to seventy-one, where a ladder waited to take him to ninety-one.

The atmosphere was heating up as the crowd thumped their metal hands and clapped: *boom-boom-chit, boom-boom-chit*. The two Zogs rolled high and progressed up the board, but the pirate and James were still in the lead, both dodging a snake's drop. Each roll went quicker and quicker as the excitement grew. James jumped onto a snake and zipped down to seventy-nine from ninety-eight.

'So close, yet so far!' he exclaimed, as he watched the pirate go down as well.

The Zogs were hot on their heels now. James held his dice tightly in his hand. Deep breaths didn't help as he looked at the next cube with its ladder up to the winning position. He heard the pirate clap in time with the crowd and even Captain Zog was stomping along to the beat.

'One!' they all shouted. 'ONE!'

James held the dice up for everyone to see. The crowd went silent. He closed his eyes and let it fall, listening for the familiar sound of it rolling to a stop. He looked down to the ground and then up to the sky. A firework shot into the air and a burst of colour illuminated the stadium.

He'd done it!

James had won. He'd get to go home and tell everyone about this adventure *and* the green Zogs would get a new time-warp cruiser! The pirate dashed through the doorways that linked the cubes and gave James a big hug.

'Well done, lad!' he cheered.

Everyone whooped and shouted as James climbed up the final steps. Standing there, he saluted Captain Zog and his team. He kissed his dice, then finally descended back to the bottom.

Once all of the contestants were gathered, Captain Zog nudged the red Zog out of the way and gave

James a silver egg-shaped trophy.

Then he addressed the crowd. 'All hail, the supreme intergalactic champion of Snakes and Ladders!'

The crowd repeated the words so loudly that James had to put down his prize and cover his ears – but that didn't stop him grinning. And in that moment, the red Zog extended his robotic arm and snatched the trophy.

James's mouth hung open in shock. Then he closed it again with a snap. 'Hey!' he yelled.

The other Zogs began to fight the red Zog, but he clung on to the trophy for all he was worth. They pulled. He pushed. It was like an enormous rugby scrum. But the red Zog just wouldn't let go.

'Stop!' James commanded the group at last.

Everyone looked at him.

'We'll roll for it,' he challenged the red Zog, and showed two dice in his hand. 'Highest roll wins the whole game.'

The red Zog hesitated, then wobbled yes. With the trophy in one hand and a dice in the other, he rolled quickly. Four. He scowled.

James took his time, then flicked the dice into the air. All eyes traced its path as it bounced across the floor, then spun for what seemed like an eternity. James chewed his lip. Two. No, one. Then it landed on a five. It was over, once and for all.

James nodded slowly to the red Zog and opened his hand. Reluctantly, the red Zog placed the trophy back where it belonged.

The celebrations began; jets of fireworks streamed across the sky, music boomed around the stadium and a giant hologram of the winners hovered in the air. The green Zog captain jumped up and down. And then, when everyone had calmed down at last, James made sure to bow to the big red Zog as a sign of respect, and asked if he would like to play again, but for fun instead. The red Zog wobbled a reluctant agreement and off they went to start again. They played and played until everyone was so tired that even the snakes started snoring like the pirate.

Then the captain came and got James, the pirate and his kangaroo. They gave one last wave to all of the Zogs in the stadium and then the ceiling of the spaceship appeared back in place.

For the first time since they had arrived, it was quiet. James didn't realise the ship had taken off until the pirate started twizzling in mid-air. The ship's hum grew louder, making him feel lightheaded. Then all too quickly, gravity kicked in and the boy heard the familiar whoosh of the door. He shook his new friend's hand and scratched the sleeping kangaroo's head.

'Goodbye,' he said.

And then there he was – he'd been beamed back to his bedroom, where it had all begun. He squinted in the darkness, listening to the tick-tock of the hallway clock.

'Did that really just happen?' he whispered as he hid his trophy in his pants draw.

'Indeed.'

James recognised the captain's voice.

'Thank you for all the fun,' James said as he scrambled back into bed.

But he didn't feel sleepy at all, especially as he could see that the captain and the other Zogs were still wobbling in excitement. Wrapped in his duvet, he waved as the Zogs started to disappear.

Then he sat up. 'Wait!' he called. He didn't have an answer to his question! 'Why did you choose a Pirate and me to compete for you?'

A quiet voice echoed. 'We've always wanted to meet a pirate from planet Earth, and you were the champion of Snakes and Ladders in your school. It was a logical choice. Until next time, Earthling James.'

James lay back and looked at his ceiling. Then he got up, grabbed his telescope and just managed to see the Zogs' spaceship disappear into the night. Meanwhile, in another country called Australia, a sleeping kangaroo suddenly appeared in his mother's pouch. His eyes lazily opened for a moment, and then he drifted back into his dreams.

AI Cat OnE

Tora slid open the heavy metal door. She winced as it screeched on its runners, and made a mental note to get more grease. Bright sunlight spilled into the shipping container that had been her home for as long as she could remember. Posters she'd found in shipwrecks covered the wavy corrugated metal walls. Tora dodged through the piles of broken electronics and sat at her workbench for a moment. Littered with tools and careworn manuals, the pitted surface had a half-repaired circuit board sitting in the middle. She turned it over in her hands. *Uncle Chen will be mad if I don't fix it soon*, she thought, but then her stomach groaned; it wanted lunch before anything else.

Flicking the switch on the generator, Tora waited

for the box to buzz. It was powered by sunlight – *solar*, Uncle Chen called it. A green screen lit up, showing 87 per cent charge. *That's good,* she thought. *Enough juice for a while.* The lamps overhead and on the workbench blinked to life, and a small circle of white light beamed onto her unmade bed. The light stretched out in the form of a cat that leapt over to where Tora stood.

'You've been gone a looooong time,' purred a curious little voice.

'Of course I have, Catone. You know I have lessons in the morning.'

Tora bent down and pretended to stroke the white fur. She'd learnt quickly not to let her hand pass through the projected light. *It breaks the sense of reality when you tinker with a hologram,* Uncle Chen had warned when he gave it to her.

Since then, Catone and Tora had become the best of friends and Catone was the only family Tora knew, apart from Uncle Chen.

'That's not the point,' Catone carried on. 'You said it yourself – lessons are dull. Besides, I can show you everything you need to know from my memory bank.'

Tora had heard it all before. She let Catone carry on complaining as she rummaged in her food cupboard and prepared a thin soup on the stove to eat with some stale bread.

The cat sat on his haunches. 'You've got a black smudge on your nose.'

Tora felt self-conscious and pulled out a cracked mirror from one of the workbench draws. She gazed at her oval face, framed by long straight black hair, and lifted her chin to get a better look. Catone was right. A dark smudge ran down the side of her nose. *How long has that been there?* She thought about the other children in the classroom staring at her this morning.

The battery-powered alarm clock next to her bed beeped, bringing her back to the present.

'It's 12.25 p.m. already! I have to go to work.' Tora went to turn off the power switch.

'School. Work. School. Work,' Catone moaned, tapping a ball made of light onto the floor. 'No time for play. Leave me on today. I want to explore under the workbench.'

Tora felt a pang of guilt. Uncle Chen wouldn't like

it if she left the power on. *A waste*, he called it. *But Uncle Chen doesn't need to find out*, she convinced herself before nodding with a smile.

Tora stepped out and shut the sliding door behind her. All around, thousands upon thousands of shipping containers were piled up on top of each other, all of them linked by a maze of walkways. This was Salvage City, sheltered in a steep valley facing a vast ocean.

Tora touched the thick cables that were fixed to the railing and imagined the power thrumming through them. Smaller links ran off into all the homes on her row, providing them with rationed electricity and water. Some people were lucky enough to have their own generator and water-collection unit. Tora was one of them, but only because of Uncle Chen.

The door next to hers opened, and Tora's neighbour stepped out. His wide mouth stretched into a smile, showing his missing front teeth. His wispy hair looked as wild as ever.

'Mooornin,' he croaked.

'Afternoon,' she corrected.

'Well, it's morning somewhere, you know.' He pushed his thick round glasses up his nose.

'Yes, I suppose it is, Uncle Chen.' She rolled her eyes at the daily joke, but couldn't suppress a small smile.

'How's that circuit board coming along?' he asked, straightening himself up.

'Almost there. Catone was helping me last night with where to add the new bits.'

'Mmm. That cat. He'd better not be distracting you from *real* learning, with *your own* brain. Education is important.'

'Yes, Uncle Chen.'

'You're wearing yesterday's dungarees, Tora. Any reason?'

'I forgot to change them,' Tora replied sheepishly, thinking of the pile of dirty clothes in the corner of her container.

'Well, we've got a day of cleaning the pumps so I suppose it doesn't matter too much. I hope you're ready for some more engineering lessons. That reactor won't keep the lights on if we don't get the water in there.'

He shuffled off on his bandy legs. Tora grinned and scurried after him. She preferred this to school. She pictured her teacher shaking her finger and ordering the class not to speak. Uncle Chen and Catone were the opposite – they treated her like an equal and answered her endless questions.

The journey through the warren of corridors and stairs led them into the depths of Salvage City, where the beating heart of its engineering hissed and rattled. Lots of people were toing and froing from the city's power source, the last working reactor. It kept them alive, and in turn they looked after it. Without it who knows what they'd do?

Despite his years, Uncle Chen always seemed to be at the front of their daily competition to be the first to arrive and Tora had given up trying to work out how. The foreman was waiting for them, scanning a crumpled piece of paper.

He looked up and narrowed his eyes as they approached. 'Nice of you to turn up.'

'Here to help, as always.' Uncle Chen bobbed his head.

'This here is a map.' The foreman poked a fat finger at the paper.

'I am familiar with it.' Uncle Chen bobbed his head again.

'I don't care if you're familiar with it, old man. It needs to be drawn again. It's torn, and junctions A1 to G29 are wrong. I need the corrections to be marked up.'

'I think you'll find a digital copy of my mapping work from two years ago in the archive. That will be up to date.'

'Paper, Chen. We need it on paper.'

Uncle Chen pushed up his glasses and gazed levelly at the foreman's red face. Tora had seen this argument a hundred times and she thought Uncle Chen was right. Paper would get lost. Better to keep a digital copy.

'Fine.' The foreman lost the battle of wills and folded the paper away. 'I was down on Block 4 yesterday. Something odd was happening there, but my crew fixed it. Now there are some leaks on Block 5. I need you to fix them.' The foreman's smile didn't reach his eyes. 'Your little rat Tora might need to help. Lots of small openings.'

Tora bristled. How dare he call her a rat! But Uncle Chen accepted the assignment and shuffled her away before she could say anything.

They set to work. The hours ticked by as they visited each reported leak and applied their knowledge to fix the problem. Each time Uncle Chen muttered to himself, 'It's not right – this shouldn't be leaking.'

Towards the end of their shift, Tora asked for a dinner break, and Uncle Chen produced his usual boiled egg and spring onion rice balls.

As they ate, the foreman stomped down the walkway, boots clattering. 'Chen? Chen?' he spouted. 'Block 6. We need you. At the back. Bring the rat.'

Tora wrapped up her uneaten food. She knew better than to let her hunger get in the way if there was something wrong with Block 6. It was the last set of control valves before the reactor and that meant trouble. Together they jogged towards the problem. Amber lights flashed and steam hissed across the corridor in pencil-thin jets. Uncle Chen passed Tora a set of thick gloves before turning the nearest stopcock. The steam stopped, but the pipes groaned.

'Tora, follow me,' he instructed.

The foreman hovered in the background, unsure what to do.

'Quick, girl,' said Uncle Chen. 'We don't have a lot of time to release the pressure valve.'

Tora panicked. 'I don't know what that is, Uncle.'

An alarm drowned out his reply. Tora covered her ears, but kept her attention on her uncle's face. The lines on his brow grew deeper and sweat snaked down his cheeks. He fished out a hammer and pointed to a crawl-way under the stopcock he'd just turned.

The foreman picked her up and shouted in her ear impatiently.

'He's asking you to go down there,' he bellowed over the alarm. 'You need to turn the red lever down. Use the hammer if you have to!'

Tora didn't need telling twice. Steeling herself against the deafening sound, she grabbed the hammer and wriggled free of the foreman. The pipes were hot to touch, but thankfully the gloves protected her hands as she pulled herself through.

There it was – the red lever – just as Uncle Chen had tried to say. Tora tugged at the plastic-covered handle, but it was stiff. There wasn't enough room to swing properly, but Tora did her best to hit the lever with the hammer head. It moved. She did it again, then gave it a firm yank. The stuffy space instantly grew cooler as a rush of cold water whooshed through the pipes. Tora repeated one of Uncle Chen's lessons: *cold after hot can crack the thickest pipe if you're not careful.* But it seemed OK. Tiredness washed over her. She crawled out and joined the others.

'Time for home,' said Uncle Chen, giving her shoulders a squeeze. 'You did good.'

Tora stopped outside her container. Uncle Chen had asked her to wait outside as he disappeared into his own place, which was full of mysterious old technology. *Like Aladdin's cave of wonders,* she thought. The walkway lights began blinking out as the power conservation timer kicked in. Her eyes adjusted to the soft glow of starlight as Salvage City shut up for the night.

Uncle Chen reappeared, his skinny frame masked by a thick duffle coat, and offered her a small black metal rectangle. 'I was saving this for a special occasion,' he smiled. 'Now seems as good a time as any.'

Tora took it from him. She knew it must be

something from before the Bright Day; it always was with Uncle Chen. But what? She rolled the object over in her hand. It was incredibly light, and had a spot for a thumb print.

'It's a special remote control,' explained Uncle Chen. 'It will allow you to take Catone out of the container, if you wish. But use it with caution; people will be jealous. Also, just like the lights, it needs juice to keep going.'

Tora accidentally popped the end of the remote control off.

'Yes, that's it,' Uncle Chen confirmed. 'You plug that end into the projector for Catone. It will charge the remote control. See that blue light?' He pointed. 'It will flash green when it's good to go.'

Tora's curiosity quickly turned to excitement. She could finally spend time outside with Catone! Her mind buzzed with all the possibilities.

'Thank you,' she whispered.

Uncle Chen waved her away. 'Be sure to get a good night's sleep. You've got school in the morning.'

Tora bobbed her head and opened her container, eager to try the remote. Light spilled out onto the walkway. Of course – she'd left it on! Uncle Chen rolled his eyes as she disappeared inside.

'Catone? Catone, where are you?'

'Here, obviously.' He poked his head out from below the workbench.

'I've got something. Uncle Chen gave it to me.' Tora piled up the old manuals on her desk in one corner to free up some space, then pulled out the box that housed Catone's memory. The green light on the top was square, like the remote control's. Same tech, she realised. Feeling around the edges for the slot, Tora explained what the remote control would allow Catone to do.

He listened patiently, then tilted his head. 'It's on the front – bottom left-hand side.'

Tora took the cap off and plugged in the remote control. Above her head, Catone's projector whirred, then beamed its screen onto the wall. A glowing blue circle rotated in the middle of the screen. 'Please wait…' a boring voice advised. Then the information on the screen changed, and the voice droned on: 'This is a motion upgrade for Artificial Intelligence Cat Version 1.1. Please confirm you wish to proceed. This may take several moments, after which a restart is required.'

The 'Proceed' option was highlighted in a blue box.

Tora glanced at Catone, who was washing his head with his paw.

'Proceed,' she instructed.

A tick appeared on the screen. Catone was about to say something, but then flashed out of existence.

'Catone?' Tora said, an edge of panic in her voice.

'What?' the cat replied as he appeared back in the same position, eyes trained on her.

'Upgrade complete,' the voice confirmed.

'Do you feel any different?' asked Tora.

Catone walked in a circle. 'Not really. Shall we try it?'

Tora pulled out the remote control and dashed across to the container door. 'Come on.'

Catone leapt over and placed a tentative paw on the walkway. It didn't disappear like it had the last time he tried.

'It worked!' Tora exclaimed. 'Let's get on the roof.'

She scrambled up a makeshift ladder and looked down behind her for Catone, but he wasn't there.

'What are you looking at?' he asked from above her.

'Oh! I was looking for you. How did you get up before me?'

'I don't know. I thought about being on the roof and then here I was.'

Tora shrugged, then sat down and looked out at

the clear sky. Her stomach rumbled, so she took out Uncle Chen's spring onion rice balls and hard-boiled eggs from her pocket and wolfed them down.

Then she turned to Catone. 'You know your memory banks?' she asked.

'Yes. What about them?'

'Well, do you think they're a bit like those crystal orbs in my favourite storybook? You know, the ones where he stores the memories.'

Catone searched his database of information then replied, 'I suppose they could be. It's just a story though.'

'Yeah.' Tora sighed before continuing. 'But what if there was some truth in it? What if the Memory Thief managed to create some sort of memory storage…?'

'So what?' said Catone, with a dainty flick of his paw. 'He'd never be as good as me, anyway.'

Tora smiled. 'I just can't help wondering if the magic I read about in those old books is a bit like the technology gadgets we have today – like you, for example. Even now, the foreman doesn't like using Uncle Chen's gizmos. I bet he's afraid – probably calls them magic when it's really something else.'

Catone jumped up and started playing with a projected ball, clearly bored by the conversation.

'Come on, let's go somewhere!' he suggested.

Off they went, using Catone's new capability to explore the surrounding walkways, before finally going to bed.

The next morning, when the alarm clock beeped, Tora tried to cover her head with a pillow.

'Time to get up.' Catone poked his head through her blankets. 'I want to see this school place.'

Tora grunted, then sluggishly slid out of sleep into another day. Picking yesterday's dungarees and her last fresh T-shirt, she got dressed and made some toast for breakfast. Then she unplugged the fully charged remote control for Catone and went outside. She yawned, then plodded in the opposite direction to work, while Catone peppered her with questions about everything they saw along the way.

The entrance to the school looked like every other container but with a simple sign above it. Tora switched off the remote control and stuffed it in her pocket. Inside, metal chairs and workbenches were lined up across the room. At least a dozen children were chatting and playing at the front. Tora slid into a chair at the back and waited for the lesson to begin.

The teacher popped through another door and gave out thin tablets on a first come, first served basis. Tora hated that – it meant that if she wanted a good one, she'd have to go to the front and make herself known. *Education is important*, she heard Uncle Chen say. The tablets were old technology, but easy to repair with all the spare parts in Salvage City; you touched the screen and it came to life with buttons and information. Tora picked herself up and walked to the front to collect hers, but as she did so, Jin, one of the boys, stuck his leg out – and she tripped.

'Watch out for the floora, Tora,' he teased.

Tora glowered at him. The others all sniggered, while the teacher told her to hurry up.

The first lesson was mathematics and science. Tora tried not to yawn her way through the exercises, which she'd done a million times before. She could complete them in her sleep.

Then Catone appeared next to her bag. 'What's

happening? I'm bored. It's more exciting under the workbench than here. Let's go outside, or home.'

'Shhh,' Tora hissed. 'How'd you turn on? I didn't press the remote. The teacher might see you.'

Catone jumped onto the chair next to her, ignoring her question. 'I heard what you're learning. Basic stuff. Electrical engineering is more exciting. You know, like that circuit box you're fixing.'

'Yes.' Tora tried to look like she was concentrating as one of the other girls glanced back in her direction. She reached into her pocket and pressed the button on the remote control.

But Catone looked up at her. 'I don't want to go. I'm going to sit here. The answer to that question is 3.14.'

Tora suppressed her frustration. 'I know the answer, Catone. Why won't you turn off?'

The teacher announced it was break time and the screech of metal shuffling on concrete filled the room.

'What's that?' asked the girl from before, pointing at the cat.

Tora froze, struggling to remember the girl's

name. She knew she was Jin's sister. *I shouldn't have brought Catone*, she realised. What if the teacher comes over? Catone might be taken away, or worse…

The girl stood there waiting and Jin sauntered over.

And then Catone spoke up. 'I'm Catone,' he told the girl, licked his paw without looking at her.

Tora stood between them, awkwardly silent.

'I'm Ji-Yoo. This is my brother, Jin.'

'I know who you are!' Catone said pointedly at Jin. 'You tripped my friend. A nasty thing to do.'

How did he know? Tora wondered.

'Yeah, well, you're a stupid bit of old tech. Look!' Jin stepped over and rubbed his hand through Catone's face. It went all fuzzy. 'Just a hologram. Nothing is better than a human. That's what my father says. You're not even real. Stupid fake cat.'

Anger boiled up inside Tora. He couldn't say that about her only friend. She pushed Jin, and Catone disappeared and then reappeared on the floor behind him when Jin fell through him.

'By the way, the answers you whispered to your

sister were wrong,' the cat told him. 'You should ask Tora. She is smarter than you.'

The teacher looked up. 'What's going on back there? Tora, are you causing trouble again? Sit down.' Tora went to reply, but got cut off by the teacher.

'No, I don't want to hear it. It's time for history. Jin, Ji-Yoo, back to your desks.'

Catone rolled his eyes and flashed out of existence, while Tora sullenly sat back in her chair and switched on her tablet.

The rest of the lesson went agonisingly slowly. Finally, the teacher called lunchtime and Tora sped out of school and back home. Uncle Chen was waiting for her this time, and Catone beamed into life by her leg.

'AI Cat One, I see you're up and about. Good mooornin',' said Uncle Chen.

The cat swished his tail dismissively. 'My name is Catone . . . and it's afternoon. You know, school is very boring.'

'We learnt about the Bright Day in history,' Tora interrupted, before Catone could cause any more trouble, 'and the towering cities that used to exist before it happened. The other children didn't believe there were so many people before.'

'Bright Day,' Uncle Chen moaned. 'My goodness, what a name to call it. Makes it sound like a holiday. It was a nuclear war, Tora! Between countries who thought they were better than everyone else. If you saw the brightness from those bombs, believe me, there'd be nothing left of you – you'd be vaporised. *Kabow! Kapeesh!* It was a tragic day and one we must never forget.'

He turned away. Tora sensed the deep hurt he always tried to hide when Bright Day came up. She suspected he'd lost someone dear to him and felt sad about it, so she tried to make him feel better. 'I know it was terrible, but now we have the safe zones and new energy tech. We're not running out of anything any more, are we?'

But Uncle Chen stayed thoughtful and quiet.

Catone trotted off down the walkway. 'Let's go or we'll be late.'

'I don't think so.' Uncle Chen pulled himself out of thoughts. 'Just Tora and me. No AI Cat One.'

Tora didn't argue. She pressed the button on the remote control and Catone disappeared from sight. Then she quickly pretended to put the gadget back in her container and went after Uncle Chen.

At the start of their shift, in the depths of Engineering, the foreman gave Uncle Chen and Tora a list of repair jobs as usual. This time some electrical control panels were sparking, so Uncle Chen consulted his personal tablet and off they went.

After a brief inspection, he scratched his hairless chin. 'It's not right,' he complained to himself before giving Tora instructions. 'Brown wire into that socket, then the blue over there and finally the earth needs to slot in there. Earth is the green and yellow one. I'll be back in a second.'

Tora looked at the four small holes, plus the three wires poking out. Earth – she knew that one; but which one was neutral again? Her hands sweated in the thick gloves she had to wear. She pinched the brown wire and began inserting it into one of the middle holes.

'It's the other wire,' Catone commented.

Tora let out the breath she was holding. 'Catone, not now.' She looked down the corridor and muttered, 'Why did I bring you? I'm an idiot.'

'It's OK. I can help. Brown is live and goes into the hole linked to the fuse. See there?' He pointed with his paw. 'Imagine if too much power goes through it. That little cylinder goes *poof*, and the rest of the panel is protected because there isn't a link any more.'

Tora sighed, then carried on working under Catone's instruction. In a matter of minutes the work was done. Rather than waiting, she flicked the power switch controlling the security doors and, hey presto! – they shut automatically, and the panel didn't spark. *I wonder what caused the problem*, she thought, as she traced a powdery white line up from the panel to the floor above.

Uncle Chen appeared with the foreman beside him. Both were frowning until they saw the working door.

'See, no problem here, Chen,' the foreman

exclaimed. 'Your little rat has sorted it.'

Tora clenched her fist. If only she was big enough she'd give the foreman what for. And then, at the mention of a rat, Catone poked his head out.

'What's that?' The foreman stepped to one side and looked down at the cat.

Tora tried to put herself in between them. 'Nothing!' she said in a light voice, but it didn't work. Her leg passed through her friend and showed the little white cat, head tilted and staring up at the foreman.

'You're a little fat, aren't you?' purred Catone innocently. 'Surprising, given the rationing that Tora mentioned. I have an exercise programme if you need some help losing weight.'

The foreman clearly didn't know whether to frown or be delighted. 'Is that an artificial intelligence stick? That's rare tech to find around here. I'm sure it's your doing, Chen,' he added accusingly.

'I'm a cat dummy and my name is...' Catone blinked out of existence as Tora turned him off in a rush and hid the remote control in her palm.

Uncle Chen stepped over, red-faced, and held out

his hand for the remote control, but the foreman grabbed the stick out of Tora's hand and pressed the button with his meaty forefinger.

'Turn on, you stupid thing. Come on.'

'You're a dummy and not my family,' Catone's disembodied voice replied. 'Go away.'

'Catone, stop!' Tora hissed, knowing he was only going to make things worse.

'You belong to whoever holds this stick.' The foreman waved it around.

'I do not belong to anyone,' Catone grumbled.

'He shouldn't argue like that – it's one of the laws that stupid old tech follows – don't disobey your master. You're a thing, not a person. Ah, this is rubbish.' He tossed the remote control to the ground. 'It's broken, little rat,' he said to Tora, before walking off.

Catone appeared next to Tora's leg. 'I don't like that man.'

Tora ignored Catone for a second. She was looking up at Uncle Chen's stern face. He was angry.

'Go home,' he whispered.

She began to protest, but he stopped her. 'Now.

I'll deal with you later, Tora. And switch off that cat.'

The pair sat on Tora's container roof and looked out at the sea stretching into the distance. Clouds were starting to roll in, a thick layer of grey over the dark expanse of water.

'Looks like a storm.'

'Shut up, Catone,' Tora snapped. 'Haven't you caused enough trouble today? They almost always pass us by. I'm starting to think Uncle Chen never should have given me your upgrade.'

She folded her arms. Catone tried to lightly tap her crossed leg, but his paw went straight through it. Something held her back from speaking to him. *Just a hologram*, the foreman had said. But he felt like so much more than that. Were there really old technology laws he had to follow? She wasn't sure. Tora decided it was time for bed. Uncle Chen must have been busy at work, because he still hadn't come back.

Rain peppered the roof of the container. Catone looked up from his investigation under the workbench as thunder rumbled in the distance. *I knew I was right*, he thought, absently nosing through a discarded pile of clothes as he explored his new ability to move without the projector. That storm is coming here. Suddenly the container shook a little as thunder growled again. Tora turned over in her sleep.

Catone's whiskers prickled. *It's getting closer.* He decided to go up to the roof to see what was happening. Huge raindrops hammered the top of the container. Lightning struck Salvage City in three places at once, followed by a crash of thunder. Something made him want to curl up with Tora all of a sudden. He imagined himself on the blanket, and there he was.

Tora stirred. The container shook again as an almighty thunderclap broke overhead. An alarm blared out, and the plastic box in the top corner of Tora's container began flashing red. She held her hand over her ears against the deafening noise.

Uncle Chen appeared in the doorway, looking

even more unkempt than usual. He pulled her out of bed and pushed clothes against her chest. 'Come on. It's the reactor. Something's wrong. We've got to go now!'

Catone knew better than to say anything and flashed himself out, back into the remote control. Tora didn't need to blink away the sleepy fog, like she usually did in the morning – her body was ready to burst into action. Rushing after Uncle Chen through the maze of walkways, something told her to reach into her pocket. Catone's remote control was still there! For a brief moment she thought about going back, but there wasn't enough time. She'd just have to hope he didn't pop up.

The foreman was standing at the main entrance to the engineering levels in the middle of a crowd of people, all shouting and rushing around. The alert was sending ripples of red light across everyone. Tora gripped Uncle Chen's hand tighter. She'd never seen everyone in such a panic. Thunder boomed overhead.

Then one of the crew spotted them. 'Chief Engineer Chen. Thank goodness. The reactor is losing water pressure. We've got ten minutes before it explodes. We've begun the evacuation of Salvage City.'

Uncle Chen pushed his glasses up his nose. 'Where are the main issues?'

'The pumps have exploded – on Blocks 5 and 6, where the leaks were spotted earlier this week.'

Tora's eyes widened. What if this had happened because of her? She was only there yesterday. What if she'd accidentally done the wrong thing?

The foreman stepped forward.

'We think the control panel is broken next to the main water tank, but it wasn't struck by lightning. That's all we know.'

Uncle Chen looked at the foreman for a second.

'It's his fault, I bet,' Catone whispered to Tora.

'Sshh,' Tora replied.

'Foreman,' Uncle Chen began. 'Have your crew dress in protective gear, not pyjamas. Prepare to work through into tomorrow. I'll be going to the water tank to fix it, then you'll need to repair the reactor.'

'Look, just because you're the chief engineer doesn't mean you can boss us around.'

Uncle Chen said nothing. He looked down his glasses at the foreman and waited for him to accept that the previous crew had got it wrong.

'But... but... but... my crew! They repaired the panel at the main tank,' protested the foreman, flustered. 'It must be the lightning...'

Uncle Chen raised an eyebrow before pulling out his tablet. He wasn't backing down.

'Fine. Go,' the foreman ordered, accepting defeat.

Uncle Chen and Tora left the rest of the engineers. Several flashing exclamation marks showed the damaged areas on his map. Tora put on the special headphones he passed across, and Uncle Chen tapped the attached microphone.

'Can you hear me?' Uncle Chen's voice came loud and clear.

Tora nodded.

'Come on, Tora. We'll have to go around the back. The stairwell is flooded.'

A large T on a white sign marked their arrival at the tank. Tora took in the scene. In the middle of the room was a large cylinder, and a screen showed the water level dropping. Off to the right, the pipework was bent and steaming. To the left a walkway had fallen in a mess of twisted metal.

Uncle Chen got down on one knee and looked at Tora. 'This is going to be dangerous. We'll have to split up. I'm going to the right to stop the water flow. You'll have to crawl through that gap there.' He pointed left to the crumpled walkway. 'It's about ten metres. Then you'll see the panel on the other side of the tank. I need you to fix it.'

Tora nodded, fingering Catone's remote control, then rushed off and started crawling.

It was tight. Twice she had to wriggle through some crumpled bits of stairway with Uncle Chen buzzing in her ear. It seemed to calm them both down when he was explaining something. But then suddenly, the buzzing stopped.

'Uncle Chen?'

No reply.

'Uncle Chen? I can't hear you!' Tora banged the side of the headphones.

Still nothing.

'It's OK, Tora,' Catone reassured her. 'I'm here. The surroundings are blocking the signal. I can guide you. Uncle Chen added some additional programming.'

Tora tried to slow her beating heart and kept crawling, she didn't have time to wonder how Catone had automatically come on again. After a couple of metres, she was through the broken walkway, but there was still wreckage everywhere. How would she find the panel in time?

'Over here.' Catone appeared, a shining white beacon in the shadows.

Tora crawled over and pulled out her tool kit. The panel was black with smoke, but most of the wiring was intact. Catone jumped up on top of the panel box. A chalky white line ran up towards the top of the tank where a leak had left a mark. Water had damaged it, not lightning, Tora realised. After a deep breath she set to work, using what she had learned to replace the fuse and check the wires. Within a few moments, she was ready. She flipped the switch.

Nothing happened.

She flicked it again. No lights on the panel. It was dead.

Catone peered down at her. 'The wires behind the fuse have burnt out.'

'Now what? Shall I go back and get Uncle Chen?'

'No, it's too late for that.' Catone's tail twitched as he thought of an idea. 'We need to reroute the power through that socket there. You can plug my remote control into it and then I can talk to the computer.'

Tora fished the control out of her pocket. Reluctantly, she went to put Catone's remote control in the slot. She wished she'd worked more on that circuit board Uncle Chen had given her; it might have helped her figure out all the complicated stuff in front of her.

'Wait. There must be another way.'

'There isn't,' Catone replied, calmly.

There was something in his glance that made Tora hesitate. 'Catone, you'll be OK, won't you?'

He paused before replying. 'The power might be too much for me. I might not come back.'

Tora felt a tear track down her cheek. She wanted to say *No! I order you not to do it!* But she knew it was pointless to argue. If they didn't sort this out, the reactor would explode and all of them would die.

'Family is important. You taught me to protect it. You and Uncle Chen are my family.' Catone nuzzled her hand, his whiskers passing through her.

She plugged him in.

'Goodbye, Tora.'

Catone disappeared and the patch panel lit up, its inner workings buzzing. A big clunk echoed from above and water flowed down the pipework. Tora stared fiercely at the remote control, willing the green light to come on. The moment stretched out.

Nothing. Catone was gone.

A deep well of sorrow opened in the pit of her stomach. She could hardly see through her tears. She clutched the remote control in her palm. It was very hot, but she didn't care. The burning matched how she felt.

Tora didn't know how long she sat there. At some point the wreckage was removed and Uncle Chen wrapped his arm around her before guiding her away. Engineers were rushing around, repairing the damage. The plan had worked. Everyone would be safe in Salvage City, thanks to Catone.

The storm passed and the alarm stopped, leaving it very quiet. Back at the entrance to Engineering, Uncle Chen explained the root cause of the breakdown to everyone. The previous repair work on the tank hadn't been done correctly by the foreman's crew, and that had caused the leaks in the other blocks and broken the panel. The foreman apologised sheepishly.

Tora listened but couldn't bring herself to hate the foreman, or smile as the work crews congratulated her. *Catone is the hero,* she wanted to say. *He died for us.* But could a bit of software die? The voice in her head wasn't sure. She thought of Jin mocking Catone's realness in school.

'It feels like he died to me,' she whispered to herself.

Uncle Chen looked down, said a few words to the

others, then guided her home.

At their container doors, Uncle Chen got on his knee and pushed up his thick glasses.

'I'll miss AI Ca—' He paused. 'Catone, as well.'

Tora kept looking at her feet.

'He was special. I see that now. The way he could make his own choices. I don't understand how he did it, but I suspect he was more than just a bit of software.'

'He wasn't just my friend, he was part of my family.'

'Yes,' Uncle Chen replied, softly. 'Come on, let's get some food in my container.'

Tora shook her head. 'No. I want to be alone.'

She slid open her door and left Uncle Chen outside. It felt good to shut out the world. Just her.

She fiddled with Catone's remote control for a while, then sat at her workbench. As she was mulling over the events of the day, the green light on Catone's old black projector box began to flash. Something drove her to plug in the remote control.

The green light stopped, then turned blue, and the projector whirred into action.

Tora turned her chair and looked up at the screen. White letters spelt, 'Welcome to the default set-up for AI Cat One. This is where you decide how you'd like your AI to be, from kitten to cat.' It told her what she already knew: the Catone she loved was truly gone.

FUR COLOUR?
▸ GINGER
BLACK & WHITE
SEAL POINT
TORTOISESHELL

Tiredness swept over her. She switched off the projector, crawled into bed and let sleep take her away.

Later that night, while Salvage City was dark and silent, the projector light flashed blue, then amber, then green. The default menu loaded onto the screen, the 'Let's start' option highlighted as before. Something selected it and a green tick appeared in the middle. Then a new message popped up: 'Loading options'. Tora opened her bleary eyes as the projector announced in a familiar voice, 'I want to be ginger this time, with one green eye and one blue.'

*If you enjoyed the stories in this book,
look out for Atticus Ryder's next collection.
Read on for a taste of what's to come ...*

DEsert Lily

'As promised, I have found yer business ledger,' Taffy stressed with his gruffest voice. He held a leather-bound book gingerly between his thumb and forefinger. Gloopy liquid dripped off its edges. He placed the book on the table and a gust of wind coated the cover with sand. Taffy rolled his eyes; this wasn't going quite as he'd planned. A small camel bleated, nibbling Taffy's ginger beard when he didn't respond.

'Not now Gerty.' Taffy pushed the camel's muzzle back.

The merchant sitting opposite him tried to turn some of the stuck-together pages then her face creased into a frown. 'It's drenched in camel's spit. All the ink is running. I couldn't tell you if this was a library book or my business records for the last month!'

Taffy brushed off her doubt with a question.

'Will ye be paying the finder's fee in coin or water?'

The merchant tutted and stood up to leave. Taffy looked down at the ledger. His stomach grumbled.

'I'll settle for lunch,' he gave a lopsided grin.

The merchant swept her scarf around her head and sauntered off into the crowded street. Two fat merchants at the next table sniggered. He gave them a pointed smile just as Gerty snatched up the ledger and trotted after their recently departed patron.

'Gerty!' Taffy sighed. 'She knows you've found it old girl.'

Gerty turned back and flared her nostrils, covering the book in yet more slobber. Taffy rubbed her humps sympathetically before gently tugging the book out of her mouth.

'Come on. Let's see if I can get us some discounted lunch at the Wavy Dune.'

The midday sun beat down. Taffy scratched under his eye patch, then shifted it to the other eye as he entered the Wavy Dune. It was dim inside. He could make out at least fifteen other patrons hunched in the shadows. The innkeeper looked up while his hands continued to clean a mug.

'You know people will catch on that the eye patch is fake if you keep switching it.'

Taffy slumped onto a stool, spun his last coin on the tabletop and watched it slow to a stop.

'Won't buy you a lot,' the innkeeper pointed out. 'Since the water shortage last week prices have tripled. You can polish the brass as additional payment while I'm cooking.'

'Ye be too kind fer yer pirate guest.' Taffy gave a thumbs up.

'And you don't need to keep up that accent. I know you're just another one of us trying to get by.'

Taffy felt his cheeks get hot, embarrassed.

'Thanks,' he replied in his normal voice.

The kitchen was in its usual mess – every surface strewn with knives and forks, pots and pans, fresh vegetables, plates and cloths. The innkeeper handed him a rag and several brass things. Gerty poked her head through the open back door.

The innkeeper sighed. 'How many times do I

have to tell you? No pets.'

'But Gerty isn't a pet.' Taffy grinned. 'She is a very efficient homing device.'

The innkeeper rolled his eyes and started chopping some vegetables, throwing the trimmings in Gerty's grateful direction. Taffy rubbed a brass oil lamp in-between mouthfuls of fresh bread.

'Innkeeper, service,' someone hissed from the front of the inn. Taffy peered around the corner. A tall skinny man slouched over the bar while picking his nose.

'Good day. What can I get you?' The innkeeper replied.

The man sneered. 'A free jug of water for a start. His Lordship will be thirsty.'

Another man, dressed the same but shorter and fatter, pulled some chairs over to one of the corner tables. 'Get some bread as well Damper.'

'You heard him,' Damper snarled.

Taffy watched the innkeeper's tight-lipped nod as he put yesterday's bread in a bowl, before filling a jug with water and setting down a single cup. At that moment, another man swept aside the dangling beads at the door and waltzed in, his silk clothes swishing. The room went quiet. Taffy watched the man focus on the innkeeper.

'Excuse Damper and Bucket. They can be,' his sickly sweet voice paused, 'overzealous.'

'It's always a pleasure to have his Lordship Vane visit.' The innkeeper smiled, but it didn't reach his eyes.

'Mmm.' Lord Vane dismissed him with a wave of his hand, then settled down at the table and pulled out a ream of paper with a quill. Someone coughed. Taffy shifted his eye patch before settling down two tables away from Lord Vane – he sensed an opportunity.

'Smiler, where are you?' Lord Vane called out.

A large mud-coloured lizard padded into the room. In its mouth it held a clump of long grass. A rare sight in the desert. The lizard's claws scratched long lines in the dirt floor as he ambled over to where his master sat. The spines lining his back quivered and he spat out the grass, flicking out his tongue.

'You will be wondering why I am here.' Lord Vane addressed the room. 'An object has been stolen from me. I will give fifty barrels of water to the person who recovers it.'

Lord Vane paused as a wave of murmurs rippled around the room. Taffy's jaw dropped – fifty water barrels! He tapped his fingers as he counted up how many coins that would be: twenty jugs to a barrel, four coins for a jug: 4,000 coins! I could buy the Wavy Dune outright he thought.

Lord Vane motioned for quiet. 'In addition to this handsome reward you will also be the hero of this town, because the theft of this object has also caused the drought we are all suffering. Once the object is returned I will be able to decrease prices. Now step forward.'

Special Thanks

I would like to express my sincerest gratitude to my wife, Anna. Quietly and confidently she has encouraged me to explore my creative spirit. Together we've enjoyed my characters' adventures, laughed at their antics and cried through their struggles. Anna has spurred me on to write more than I thought possible! Please Anna, just *one more* read-through of the 3rd draft and we'll be done, *promise* (at least on the latest story in my next collection).

To Paul Samuel, a posthumous thank you. As a mentor and a friend, your urge to *just do it* gave me the push I needed. I wouldn't be the person I am today without your counsel.

Finally, to those that took my scribbles and sketches and made them into a published book, John, Caroline, Clair, Gill and the wider team at Whitefox. Your suggestions, patience, insight and professionalism made this possible. Thank you.

About
Atticus Ryder

Atticus Ryder is a writer and illustrator. Born and raised in the countryside, he has been a lifelong fan of practical jokes, Lego, colourful adventures and above all else a good story. Atticus currently lives in the big smoke (London) with his family, taps friends on the opposite shoulder and glues coins to the floor.

Back in secondary school Atticus had the good fortune to bump into Derik the Dragon, whose tale helped him to win a prize in a short story competition. Over the years other characters like Albert the Dancing Troll, Old Man Ferris and Reginald the Toad gave him their stories to tell – now they're here for you.

P.S. He has just met some more travellers from magical moments between the sunset and the moonrise. Look out for their stories in his next collection...

www.twilightcat.co.uk